NORWICH BOOKF
Olson, Melissa F.
Switchback /

W9-DFQ-581

GUERNSEY MEMORIAL LIBRARY

0 00 04 0301038 2

Guernsey Memorial Library
3 Court Street
Norwich, NY 13815
www.guernseymemoriallibrary.org

SWITCHBACK

MELISSA F. OLSON

A TOM DOHERTY ASSOCIATES BOOK

NEW YORK

This is a work of fiction. All of the characters, organizations, and events portrayed in this novella are either products of the author's imagination or are used fictitiously.

SWITCHBACK

Copyright © 2017 by Melissa F. Olson

All rights reserved.

Cover images from Getty Images
Cover design by Fort

Edited by Lee Harris

A Tor.com Book
Published by Tom Doherty Associates
175 Fifth Avenue
New York, NY 10010

www.tor.com

Tor® is a registered trademark of
Macmillan Publishing Group, LLC.

ISBN 978-0-7653-9827-7 (ebook)
ISBN 978-0-7653-9828-4 (trade paperback)

First Edition: October 2017

Switchback

Prologue

At twenty-eight, Terry Anson wasn't particularly impressed with his lot in life.

Like everyone else in Switch Creek, Terry had left town for college, where he spent the next three years telling anyone who would listen that he was a "B&P" major, meaning, of course, "beer and pussy." The joke always got plenty of laughs—or at least, it did in his mind—but by the end of his junior year, Terry had to face the fact that even a thorough and intensive analysis of B&P was not, in fact, a viable path to graduation.

His parents had hired tutors, of course, as they had for Terry's two older siblings, but Terry shared the same fundamental blind spot as so many members of his generation: He did not truly believe he could fail at anything. Therefore, while he wasn't completely stupid, the possibility that his disinterest in studying would result in an actual, life-altering consequence like flunking out of college did not occur to him. Not until it was too late.

The spring after his junior year, Terry told his friends he had decided to take a year off, and by midsummer he'd convinced himself that this was, in fact, the truth. He was taking a break from school, simple as that. For the next few months, his days and nights were occupied with video games, beer, and the weight room at his parents' country club.

Terry could happily have gone on like this indefinitely, but in September his parents announced that his father was retiring from the money management firm in Chicago. Furthermore, they were tired of the harsh Illinois winters, and would be spending the majority of their time at the condo in Palm Springs.

This sounded like a great idea to Terry, who immediately volunteered his services as caretaker of the massive Switch Creek house. Before he could even dive into a fantasy about bringing girls from Chicago clubs back to the spacious five-bedroom, though, his parents exchanged a glance. "About that," his father said. "We're keeping this house for now, because we want to have the space for grandkids during holidays. But if you want to continue living here, you're going to need to pay rent and utilities."

"And buy your own groceries," added his mother, who had grown very tired of finding the refrigerator empty of whatever she'd been planning to make for dinner.

Terry was shocked. He looked from one to the other, waiting for a punch line, but his parents were clutching each others' hands, a sure sign that they were determined to be a united front on this matter. "What am I supposed to do?" Terry cried. "Be a stock boy at Target? How is *that* going to look to your friends at the club?"

His parents exchanged another look, and Terry realized with horror that they were prepared for this question. His father took a sheaf of papers out of his briefcase. "We've come up with another option."

Terry took the papers rather reluctantly. The top sheet read *Thank you for your interest in employment with the Switch Creek Police Department.* He looked up at his parents in confusion. "You want me to become a cop?"

"They require two years of college and two years with a law enforcement agency," his mother informed him. "Your father has called in a favor with the chief of police. Glenn will let you do your two years *with* the department, if you can pass all the tests."

Terry considered this, one athletic-sandaled foot resting on the edge of the coffee table. The idea wasn't necessarily repellent, but Terry had always assumed he'd graduate college and take a job in his dad's firm, doing . . . well, something with money. Whatever his dad and older brother did. He'd rent an expensive apartment in the Loop, spend every night with a new girl, and basically stay drunk until he hit thirty-five or so and was required to churn out grandchildren.

"This is the end of the road for us, son," added his father. "Your brother and sister are settled, and frankly, we're tired of parenting. You can do this, or you can be on your own."

"I don't care what my friends think about you working at Target," his mother put in. "I'll be in Palm Springs anyway."

"Huh." Terry rolled the idea around in his head like he was tasting a new microbrew. A beat cop? The idea wasn't exactly sexy. Then again, some girls were into guys in uniforms. And within a couple of years, surely Terry could advance up to captain or lieutenant or whatever, and eventually run the whole place. Maybe then he'd transfer over to the FBI. He could see himself in a tailored suit and expensive sunglasses, posing next to a corpse with a studious frown on his face as he spotted the crucial piece of evidence that had stumped all the locals. FBI agents had to get a *ton* of ass.

"Okay," Terry said. "I'm in."

The physical tests were a breeze, and for the first time in his life, Terry did do a little studying for the written exam. He passed with two points to spare, and very soon the department was sending him off to train at the academy. Terry's future, which he had always seen as hazy but bright, was at last decided. Beat cop to detective to chief to FBI agent. Nothing to it.

Terry muddled through the academy and his probationary years, but the only part of his job that he really enjoyed was the physical stuff. As much as he dreamed of chasing bad guys through a parkour-style maze of buildings, though, crime in Switch Creek was pretty much limited to a little embezzling and the occasional DUI. He couldn't believe how boring cops' lives were.

He did have a brief spark of renewed excitement when he was twenty-seven, and the public became aware of the existence of vampires. For once in his life, Terry followed the news fervently, and he was elated when the state of Illinois, like several other states, grew tired of Congress's indecision and declared the consumption of human blood illegal. Terry's patrols were briefly more exciting, as he told himself fantastical stories of Terry Anson, vampire hunter. He imagined catching a shade alive, which would surely let him leapfrog right over to the FBI's new vampire division.

Within a few weeks, however, Terry finally realized that shades had about as much of a presence in Switch Creek as serial killers. In fact, no cop in all of Illinois had managed to spot *anyone* breaking the new law. It was a colossal disappointment.

By then, seven years had passed without a single promotion, and Terry had begun to get angry. All of his high school friends had graduated from law school or med school—paid for by their parents, of course—secured jobs in the city, and were coming back to settle down and start families. It would be one thing if Terry were, say, the chief of police, but he was a twenty-eight-year-old beat cop. It was embarrassing as hell.

To avoid having to think too much about this, Terry began to drink, including when he was out on patrol. Little by little, the natural charm that had propelled Terry this far in life vanished, and his resentment soon turned into a suppressed rage that simmered just under the surface of all his interactions with the public.

And then in October, less than a year after the discovery of shades, his parents announced that they had decided to sell the house—which meant that Terry, who hadn't exactly been frugal with his tiny public service paychecks, would need to find himself a shitty apartment. Faced with the loss of DVR, pool privileges, and an impressive place to bring women, something dark ignited in Terry Anson. Something ready to explode.

The situation could have followed a predictable progression into alcoholism and disgrace, turning Terry Anson into another of the cautionary tales that mothers in Switch Creek told high schoolers who didn't want to study. Before that could happen, though, Terry actually managed to bully his way into the life-altering moment he'd been longing for.

That year, the Downtown Switch Creek Association had made the decision to time their Fall Festival to the high school's Homecoming weekend, which was also the same weekend of several high school reunions, including Terry's. The idea was to give an enormous push to local commerce before the holidays really took off. For Terry, though, this meant that everyone he'd ever known seemed to be back in town to rub their successes in his face. He was even assigned to patrol at the festival, which meant that everyone would see firsthand how pathetic his life was.

So Terry was already in a black mood on Thursday night as he prowled through the bustling town square in his dorky uniform. This mood wasn't at all helped by the fact that Terry himself was about three-quarters drunk.

There were people in town he hadn't so much as thought about in ten years, and every one of them had a better life than he did. Itching to avenge this injustice, Terry lashed out by writing seven jaywalking tickets and marking a number of cars for parking infractions. He was just toying with the idea of giving a town alderman a citation for public drunkenness, just for the hell of it, when he saw Aidan Kerns leaning against a tree.

Aidan had been the only person in his graduating class

who hadn't left Switch Creek at all after high school. There was something wrong with him—autism or asthma, something with an A—anyway, he'd been what Terry's mother referred to as a "troubled kid." After high school Aidan had taken a job at one of the country clubs, and he worked there to this day, washing and repairing the golf carts at night so they'd be shiny and purring for the next morning's golfers. Aidan hadn't really advanced in his job either, but unlike Terry, he'd never seemed bothered by this.

And now here he was, leaning against a tree in his pressed blue jeans and a checked shirt buttoned up to his chin, watching the live band and drinking from a bottle of beer like he was part of things. Like he belonged here as much as anyone.

In that moment, Aidan's very presence made Terry so angry that his vision seemed to pinpoint down to a dot. What the hell was the town embarrassment doing out here, walking around the festival like he was a real person? Who the fuck did that retard think he was, coming onto Terry's own territory and prancing around like he was better than him?

Terry hadn't even seen Aidan in years—that was how rarely the idiot came out of his house—but he decided he had never hated anything as much as he hated Aidan fucking Kerns.

"Hey!" he barked. A dozen people looked up in alarm, but none of them was Aidan. The idiot's disregard just fueled Terry's rage even more. "Kerns!" he shouted, and Aidan looked up with confusion. Terry stormed over.

"Oh, hello, Terry," Aidan said, his eyes dancing around, focusing on everything but Terry himself. He was wearing spotless sneakers that practically glowed in the dark, they were so white. "I haven't seen you in a while."

"What do you think you're doing here, freak?" Terry growled.

"I'm just drinking this beer." Aidan said in the same flat tone. He sniffed a little. "I smell whiskey. Are you drunk?"

Later, Terry would not remember making a decision to hit Aidan, but suddenly his fist was blurring out and colliding with Aidan's nose. The wet crunch of cartilage against his knuckles felt *great*.

"Ow!" Aidan cried, dropping the beer, his hands rushing to his face. He looked at Terry in genuine confusion. "You hit me!"

His weak voice alone was enough to make Terry draw back his leg to follow up with a kick. Before he could connect, though, his moment, the split second he'd been waiting all his life to recognize, finally appeared. Aidan's hands filled with blood, which began to run down his wrist toward his pristine shirt. Aidan looked around frantically for a napkin or cloth, but there was nothing. Panicked, he raised his wrist and licked at the line of blood like it was a dripping ice cream cone.

And time stopped for Terry Anson, as he recognized the opportunity that had fallen at his feet.

From the corner of his eye, he took in the onlookers, the festival attendees who'd raised their cell phones and started recording the moment Terry had hit Aidan. They wouldn't have taped the punch, but they had to have gotten the moment right after. The evidence was bullet-proof. Terry Anson was about to be the first cop in the state to arrest someone under the new blood consumption laws.

He would be a hero. He would be famous. He would finally fill the gap between himself and his peers, the one that had confused and frustrated him for so long. Aidan fucking Kerns had just handed him the keys to the kingdom.

Feeling a great swell of gratitude for the little weirdo, Terry took the handcuffs from his belt, grabbed Aidan's arm, and twisted him against the tree. "Aidan Kerns," he said in his best hero-cop bellow, "you are under arrest for consumption of human blood."

Everyone was watching and whispering, and in Terry's mind, they all looked impressed. It was the greatest hour of his life.

It was also the last.

Chapter 1

Lindy did not like waiting in cars.

As one of the oldest living vampires in the world, she had long since grown accustomed to the perks that came with great age—accelerated strength, speed, healing, even the ability to go out during daylight. She was aware that these advantages could easily become a crutch, but they were too much a part of her not to rely on them, especially when she was hunting.

Being stuck in a closed car in the rain, however, dulled her hearing, her sense of smell, even her vision. She felt like she was fumbling through an underground maze in the dark, and after only three hours Lindy had a new, pitying respect for her human colleagues, who had to deal with this hobbled existence all the time.

To be fair, they also had a lot more practice with stakeouts.

Lindy was parked halfway down a narrow alley, the

small, sensible car she'd "borrowed" from a neighbor wedged snugly in between a Dumpster and a brick building. It was dark enough that no one would spot the black vehicle as they walked by, but Lindy had a perfect vantage point to see the entrance to Vapors, a hookah lounge that served as one of Chicago's newest clubs. It was also rumored to be a major center for shade attacks, according to several anonymous tips that Lindy's office had received over the last two weeks.

Dealing with tips was pretty much all they had done during that time. Since the Chicago branch of the Bureau of Preternatural Investigations had broken their big case the month before—the case involving Lindy's twin brother, Hector, who had kidnapped and used up a number of innocent teenagers—the team had been overwhelmed with reports of shade activity.

With their team leader, Special Agent Alex McKenna, in Washington testifying in front of Congress, the remaining pod members had been frantically trying to respond to as many reports as they could. They'd had to bring in several floaters from the Chicago FBI headquarters just to handle the volume of phone calls and emails.

Most of it was nonsense, of course—now that Hector's very real murders had been exposed, every criminal in the world had decided "it must have been vampires" was the new "some other dude did it"—but one or two had caught Lindy's attention, including the suggestions that Vapors was more than it seemed.

Unlike the rest of the BPI squad, who were all humans, Lindy didn't particularly care if a group of shades had adopted a certain bar to hang out in, or even if they chose their feeding partners there. What interested Lindy was that two of the anonymous tips specifically mentioned seeing people carrying suspiciously shaped trash bags out of the bar at all hours. Shades didn't need to *kill* humans in order to feed—in fact, part of their whole symbiotic function with humanity was that shade saliva provided an immunity boost, which was hard to enjoy if the victim was dead. But if Hector had stayed in Chicago, and if he was still doing his experiments on shade reproduction, there would likely be more casualties. Besides, even if her brother wasn't working out of Vapors, this was a really, really bad time for another series of shade murders to come to light. The public was still outraged over the recent casualties, and anti-shade sentiment was at its highest yet. One way or another, if there were careless shades killing humans in that club, Lindy was determined to put a stop to it before it ever became public knowledge.

It was past bar close now, but people were still running in and out of Vapors, holding up umbrellas or jackets to protect themselves from the early October downpour.

They were all so *young,* Lindy thought: early to mid-twenties, the women in scandalously short skirts and sky-high heels, the men in jewel-toned button-downs, no ties, and shiny pointed shoes. Nothing about their body language had suggested shades, and Lindy wasn't ready to get out and confront them. With the rain, she'd need to be pretty close to catch their scent, and if they *were* shades, she'd give herself away, too. She could beat almost any vampire in the world in single combat, but if the building was infested with them, even Lindy could be overpowered. She decided to wait and watch.

When the human traffic *finally* began to dwindle, she checked her watch: 3:30 a.m. Something was definitely off here. No club was that hot, not on a Thursday night. Then one last man exited the building, turning to lock the door behind him. He was different from the others: late forties, silvering hair, wearing a nice suit and flashy tie. He put his keys into the lock to bolt it, huddling a little under the awning.

This was her chance.

Leaning on her speed, Lindy leaped out of the car and raced through the alley, moving so fast that the lights in the rain became a watery blur. It felt wonderful, after sitting still for so long. By the time the manager had extracted his key and turned toward the street, Lindy had simply appeared next to him. He started in surprise, and she took a quick inhale through her nose, feeling instant disappointment. He was human.

The man blinked hard, collecting himself. "What do you want?" He had a thick accent that Lindy recognized. She gave him a genuine smile. She hadn't had a chance to practice Sicilian in *ages*.

"I have heard that this was a good place to party," she said in Sicilian, putting a hand against the door as though she were a little drunk. "Have I missed all the fun?"

The man's face lit up. "You speak Sicilian."

"Not nearly as well as you," she said sweetly. "It has been *years* since I visited. But I'm so happy to meet you . . . ?"

"Tonio." He took a moment to give her body a long, slow appraisal. Lindy was wearing a long belted raincoat, not particularly sexy, but apparently he was imagining what might be underneath. "What can I do for you, Miss . . . ?"

Lindy reached up to push damp blond curls out of her face, using the opportunity to touch her tongue to one finger. She reached out and took the Sicilian man's hand in both of hers. "You can tell me what really goes on in here," she said, pushing power into the words. She held on to the hand, to keep the rain from washing away her best weapon. Shade saliva had a remarkable ability to make its victims pliant and suggestible, which the humans usually referred to as mesmerizing. Lindy couldn't really blame them for being afraid of her, given that her spit acted as both a narcotic and a truth serum.

The Sicilian blinked, confused, and Lindy saw that the question had been too broad. "Do shades hang out here?" she said, still smiling.

"Not . . . not that I know of . . . ," Tonio sputtered, looking disappointed. He *so* wanted to please her. She leaned forward and inhaled through her nose. Tonio smelled of aftershave, cologne, deodorant, expensive tequila, body odor, and grubby cash. There wasn't the slightest whiff of shade around him, nor did he smell like any of the things shades used to hide their scents.

Had she spent all these hours trapped in that metal box for nothing? "Why is the club open so late?" she asked.

"It's not really for clubbing," he explained, still in Sicilian. "We have different suppliers coming in and out, is all."

"And what," Lindy said, giving him a flirtatious smile, "do they supply, this late at night?"

"On Tuesdays we receive cocaine, Ecstasy, LSD, and Molly," Tonio said immediately.

Lindy dropped his hand. The saliva would have been fully absorbed by now, but she was disappointed. Club drugs weren't legal, but they had nothing particularly to do with shade crime, which meant there was no way they would help her find Hector. She would have to figure out a way to get this information to someone at the DEA or the local cops, but—

"And on Wednesday nights we get in the girls," Tonio added hopefully, like a man trying to impress a date with his annual salary. "You could come back. . . ."

Lindy had already started to turn away, but that brought her up short. "What girls?"

"You know," he said eagerly. "Young ones."

The bodies in the garbage bags.

Well, Lindy thought, at least the night wouldn't be a total loss. She smiled at Tonio, leaned over, and kissed him on the cheek. The large dose of saliva hit his bloodstream, and his eyes widened with desire. Oh, this one was particularly susceptible. She knew if she looked down, there would be a bulge in his pants. "Tonio," she said in a breathy voice. "I want you to get in your car and drive to the nearest police station, about seven blocks north of here. Do you know where it is?"

He nodded, frantic to please her now. "Good. When you arrive, I want you to tell the police all about the drugs and the girls. Make a full confession, but leave me out of it. In fact, the moment you arrive at the police station, you're going to forget we ever met. Do you understand?"

"Yes." He reached for her, a quick grab at her waist to

pull her close, but Lindy was expecting it. Carefully, so as not to kill him, she raised one arm and gave him a light punch to the solar plexus.

Tonio cried out and doubled up, retching. She took a step back, but he didn't actually vomit. "Go now," she said to Tonio, who turned on his heel and fled, still bent at the waist.

Sighing, Lindy trudged through the rain, back to the alley and her waiting car. So much for Vapors.

She knew she had put too much hope on finding a link to Hector here, but she was running out of ideas. Because of the downpour, and because she was preoccupied with thoughts of Hector and the horrible acts he could be committing at that moment, Lindy was nearly to her car before she saw the man leaning against it, holding a black umbrella that covered his face.

She hissed, instinctively bracing for attack, but the umbrella tipped backward, and the graying head that peered out from it was familiar: Special Agent Harvey Bartell, one of the other five members of the Chicago pod. He wore a black trench coat, and the hand without the umbrella was held up in the universal sign for "I mean no harm." As he looked at her, though, his expression changed from calm interest to fear, and the hand strayed toward his gun.

Whoops. Lindy rearranged her facial expression to

something human—and mildly annoyed. "You shouldn't sneak up on shades, Agent Bartell."

"Sorry," he said. "Didn't mean to startle you."

She stepped closer, past the rain, and inhaled his familiar scents: musty newspapers, pipe tobacco, soap, deodorant, that something else that they didn't talk about—and the remnants of fear. His pulse tripped a little, and his gaze flickered.

She raised an eyebrow. "Liar." He had wanted to see what would happen if she were taken off guard. It was a stupid decision, but Lindy understood that in his own strange way, it had been altruistic. If she attacked someone just for surprising her, Bartell would rather it be him than a member of the public.

Now he gave her a genuine grin. "Forgive me, but with the rain and the car, I thought this might be the only chance I'd ever get. Could we talk?"

She gestured toward the passenger door, and they both got into the little black car, Lindy at deliberately human speed, and Bartell in that cautious way that aging humans had, where a tiny part of their subconscious was warning them to go slow so as not to break a hip.

"I'd ask how you tracked me down, but I suppose I have the answer right here," she said tiredly, holding up her wrist. The bracelet gleamed in the dim light from the dash. It was expensive, nearly unbreakable, and contained the best tracking device the Bureau had access to. Lindy hated it, even if she had to admit it did go with everything.

"Noelle owed me a favor," Bartell said, unembarrassed. Noelle was the FBI technician who had been tasked with maintaining the bracelet. "And I wanted to talk to you without the others."

"What about?"

"This." He gestured toward the club entrance. "You shouldn't be out here, Miss Frederick. Not alone."

"Oh?" She turned her body sideways, finally giving him her full attention. That was . . . well, it was cute. "You think I can't handle some drug-dealing pimp in Prada? He's not even a shade."

He chuckled. "I know I wasn't there when you guys went after Hector, but I've heard the stories. I'm not worried about your personal safety."

"Then what *is* your objection?"

"The way you're going about it." His features softened. "I know Alex has been gone, and we're scrambling all over the place to keep up with these reports. But eventually, someone else is going to notice that you're going out alone, without telling anyone."

"As you said, I can handle myself."

"That's not the point. You agreed to work for the BPI, Miss Frederick." Involuntarily, she glanced down at the silver bracelet. She hadn't exactly signed on by choice. Bartell followed her look and shrugged. "Still. It was a ballsy move, considering what you are, and a dangerous one, too. Considering all the anti-shade sentiment floating around . . ." He hesitated for a moment, then forged on. "I'm not positive that the FBI director would honor your agreement if your status became public."

This thought had occurred to her as well. Lindy's attorney had approved her federal pardon, but it had all been done in such a rush, when Hector was terrorizing teenagers in the Chicago area. Now that the ink was dry and individual states were doing their best to make life hard for shades, Lindy didn't know if she could trust anyone in the BPI above Alex. "But you must have noticed," Bartell went on, "that not one of the agents in our pod has ratted you out."

She had to admit, this was true. After the raid on the abandoned dental office, Lindy had quietly gone around to the FBI SWAT team and made sure that none of them remembered that she was more than human. It had been easy to mesmerize them to alter their reports, and she could have simply done the same thing to the six other members of the BPI pod, including their office manager. But something had held her back.

As if he read her mind, Bartell nodded. "We know you could have taken the memory from us, like you did the others. You trusted us to keep your secret, and in return, you got a degree of loyalty. Despite what you are."

"Loyalty," she echoed, a little bitterness in her voice. In the last few weeks, they'd barely spoken to her, and she often smelled fear following her around the office like a shadow. "But not trust."

Bartell opened his empty hands. "Sarah trusts you. I trust you. You saved our lives—more than that, you risked your own life to save us. And I think Alex would go to hell and back for you. The others . . ." He shrugged. "They're a little wary. It's in our nature."

"As humans?"

He smiled. "I meant as law enforcement. But yes, I suppose as humans, too. Try to see it from our perspective. All we've heard about shades so far is two hundred years of vampire stories and your brother's . . . recent activities."

Lindy winced. "I'm trying to change that."

"I know you are. You're showing us that your kind can be compassionate. But this sneaking around thing . . ." He gestured to the empty alley, the club door. "If you want the pod's trust, this is not the way to go about it."

Hmm. Lindy looked at the old agent with fresh eyes. Bartell came off as a quiet, nose-to-the-grindstone worker bee, and during the fracas with Hector and his people, he had mostly been sidelined with an injury.

Lindy had more or less dismissed him as either a threat or an ally. Perhaps he needed reevaluating.

"What would you have had me do?" She tilted her head toward the club. "This happened to be a false alarm, but the reports all claimed that the shades only used this location at night." When even young shades were awake and powerful.

"So we'd raid them at night." His voice was calm.

"This club has three entrances. Two fire escapes. About nine different rooms inside, in a pattern that seems designed to disorient the patrons so they stick around and dance longer."

"What's your point?"

An image flashed in her mind, making her flinch: Alex, bleeding out on the floor of a dirty abandoned building, his face and body slashed and dying. She'd been so *scared*. When was the last time she'd been that scared? When was the last time she'd been scared at all?

Lindy forced herself to unclench her jaw. "I can't protect all of you, not in a place like this, especially if there were multiple suspects. Some of you would get hurt, or die. Again."

A look of understanding flashed over his face. "Maybe we will," he replied, not unkindly. "But what do you think would happen to us if you *weren't* part of the team? If you weren't there at all? Because I can tell you for certain, we'd still go into that building. That's what we all signed on for. Including Alex." She gave his face a close look at that, but his expression was unchanged. "You need to trust us to do our job."

Lindy thought that over for a few minutes. He had a point, but she wasn't ready to concede completely. "You talk to me about trust," she said quietly, "but you're not exactly being open with the team either." Bartell kept his poker face, so she added, "About where you go on Friday mornings?"

Now he flinched. "You know about that?"

"I can smell it."

Bartell was too seasoned an agent to actually shudder, but even he couldn't suppress a look of discomfort. He shifted in the seat. "I'll tell them when I have to."

Lindy just nodded. "And we'll keep this"—she gestured to the alley, just as he had—"between us?"

He gave her a sad look, like a parent disappointed in their child. "You don't have to extort me, Ms. Frederick. I would have kept your secret anyway."

She tilted her head. "Fair enough," she allowed.

Bartell reached for the door. "Oh, and Harvey?" She touched his bare hand, which he pulled to his chest in alarm. He'd been properly briefed on shade security. Good. "I see that your heart is in the right place, and you want me to be part of the team. I really do appreciate that."

The smell of fear wafted in the car, though he did an excellent job of hiding it. "But?"

"But in the future, I'd be careful how you present these 'wise old mentor coaches the new girl' talks. I may look like a college student, but I was already powerful when your great-great-grandparents were conceived." She gave him her *real* smile, the one that didn't account for human flight-or-fight responses. "Try not to forget it."

He swallowed hard. "Good night, Ms. Frederick."

"See you tomorrow, Agent Bartell."

He got out of the car, and she watched him walk away on legs that shook only a little.

Chapter 2

Berta Hauptmann was going to be late to work again.

She knew for a fact that her personal nemesis, Junie Eliot, was angling for Berta's job as office and building manager for the SCPD. Junie was twenty years younger than Berta, but it was becoming apparent that she didn't want to wait another decade for Berta to retire so she could be senior dispatcher. Therefore, Junie felt perfectly justified in keeping a log of Berta's tardiness, which she periodically reported to Glenn Holbrook, the police chief. Glenn wouldn't dare fire Berta, who knew where all the bodies were buried—metaphorically—but still. It was the principle of the thing.

Berta tried hard to be punctual, but this morning had been even more rushed and frantic than usual. Berta's seven- and ten-year-old grandsons were staying with her while their mother, Berta's daughter Michelle, was in Copenhagen for work. Berta loved her grandsons, but she was out of practice with dragging grumpy kids out of bed, especially now that the darkness lasted later and later. By the time Berta had gotten the complaining boys to eat some breakfast and put on clean clothes, she was basically going to need a helicopter to make it to work on time. To make matters worse, it was Berta's day to bring in treats. She'd had to stop at the twenty-four-hour gas mart for a box of donuts that weren't going to impress anyone—not like Junie's homemade gluten-free scones from the week before. As Berta sped through the tiny downtown district—one advantage of working for the police was that Berta never got tickets—she could just picture Junie's sour, smugly pinched face, making an elaborate note of Berta's arrival time and lousy baked goods.

She pulled into the spacious lot, expecting to see only Junie's five-year-old Prius in the lot. The two of them started work an hour before the rest of the staff, and had to spend a tense sixty minutes making small talk and pretending to be civil to each other until the station officially opened at eight. On this morning, however, there were also several other cars parked in the lot. It wasn't unusual for one or two of the younger patrol officers to leave a vehicle overnight—in a village as small as Switch Creek, they would sometimes walk to a restaurant for drinks and then walk or get a ride home—but this many?

Then Berta remembered that the Fall Festival had

started the night before, and relaxed. Second watch finished at ten p.m.; they'd probably gone over to the town square as a group to have a beer before the vendors closed up for the night. Between the festival and the class reunions, the whole town had a bustling air of celebration and fun, and Berta couldn't blame the others for wanting to get in on it, especially the younger crowd. She also remembered that the chief had made Junie work a split shift the day before: She'd had to come back from five to ten, to handle any extra problems arising from the crowds in town. Junie was going to be even more of a pill than usual this morning.

Berta parked her trusty Subaru next to Junie's Prius and flung her handbag over her shoulder so she could trot toward the entry door. She kept her keychain in her hand, fumbling for the exterior door key. Of course, Junie *could* have opened the door for her, but the little harpy wouldn't lift a finger to help Berta, especially since—

Berta's thoughts sputtered out as she realized that the heavy door was, in fact, unlocked. She must have been even later than she'd imagined, and Junie had self-righteously unlocked the door. Berta gritted her teeth and tugged the handle, shoving the keys back into her purse. She pasted a bright smile on her coral-lipsticked face. She was *not* going to let Junie Eliot ruin her whole day.

"Sorry I'm—" Berta looked up from zipping the purse

shut and froze, her feet simply forgetting what forward momentum felt like. Junie Eliot was actually draped over the big desk just inside the interior door, her cheek resting on the fabricated wood. Her hands were tucked away in her lap, so all Berta could really see was the enormous rat's nest of a bun on top of Junie's head.

She'd fallen asleep at her desk! Berta snapped her mouth closed, choking down a whoop of triumph. In the three years since Junie had been hired to take over some of Berta's workload, she had never caught Junie so much as dozing. This was fantastic!

As quietly as she could, Berta set the box of donuts on her own desk opposite Junie's and dug in the side pocket of her handbag for her cell phone. She glanced around, but the entryway was empty, and no noise was coming from the short hallway leading to the offices. She raised the phone and began to silently circle to her left, working her way around the desk to capture Junie's face in the little screen. In the back of her mind, she was running through a half-dozen possibilities for the anticipated photo. Send it to the chief? Blackmail Junie to stop recording her tardiness? Or just post it on the department's Facebook page? Berta suppressed a giggle and hoped there was at least a little drool coming out of Junie's mouth. She squinted down at the screen, wishing she'd thought to put on her glasses first. She blinked fast, squinted one more time, and finally made out the big ratty bun tapering down to the greasy forehead. She framed the shot—

"Oh!" Berta dropped the phone, which clattered loudly to the shiny tile floor. The younger woman's eyes were wide open and staring, with a film of dull lifelessness. "Junie?" Berta said, stepping closer, but she could already see that the skin had a bluish tint. On autopilot, Berta's hand reached toward the neck to take a pulse anyway, just to be sure, just so she could say that she did. But her eyes caught the swath of dark pink and she fell back with a shriek.

Junie's throat had been torn away in a three-inch-wide strip that ran horizontally around her neck. There was almost no blood, just a drying pink slice of gore. The phrase *from ear to ear* rang horribly through Berta's mind, and she shuddered, all those hateful thoughts suddenly evaporating. Poor Junie. She'd been so young. And Berta had been so mean to her!

It was only then that Berta processed the fact that Junie Eliot had been *murdered*. Here, in Switch Creek. In the police station.

Wracked with guilt and shock, Berta had to fight to keep down the fiber granola bar she'd bolted on the way to the station. She looked around, but the small, pretty building was almost oppressively still. Her eyes may have been going, but Berta's ears were sharper than ever, and she heard nothing. For a moment, she just stood there, her whole attention focused on not puking. You work for the police, for pity's sake, she told herself. Get it together. Call for help.

But who? She couldn't exactly call 911. At seven a.m. the state police operator would have switched the local 911 calls back to their station, so a call from here would just result in the phone on the desk in front of her ringing.

The chief, Berta decided. He would answer his landline at home. She reached down, straining to get her cell phone, but when she held it up the screen was cracked into an obscuring spiderweb. "Oh, fudge!"

She didn't want to touch either of the two desk phones, since the whole room was now a crime scene. Mindlessly, Berta pushed her mobile back into her purse and took hesitant steps sideways toward the short hall, as though if she looked away, Junie might get up and follow her.

The hallway opened into Switch Creek's tiny excuse for a bullpen, a single large room with fifteen desks for the officers who covered the three watch shifts. Small offices were set along the right side of the room, for the chief of police, the school officer, and so on. On the left side there was a door leading to the three jail cells, which were usually empty. Thinking only of telephones, Berta headed toward the bullpen, where there would be a handset on every desk.

The room was dark. She felt along the wall for the switch, taking a small step forward—then one foot flew out from underneath her, and Berta went flying backward like the tile was ice, landing hard on her bottom. She groaned. Her tailbone aching, Berta grabbed the doorframe and used it to pull herself up. Her searching fingers found the light switch at last and flicked it on.

And then she understood why she'd slipped. The floor beneath her was marked in smears and footprints of rusty brown, tracking back and forth from the doorway where she stood to the jail cells. It wasn't much blood, all things considered. Second watch had probably arrested someone with a bloody nose. That kind of thing happened all the time, but Berta found that she couldn't make herself go look in the cells. Instead, panic rose within her, and an almost primal need to turn and flee. Berta swallowed hard and resolutely fixed her eyes on the closest investigator's desk, not ten feet away from her. If she could just get to the phone to call the chief, Berta told herself, all of this would be fine. The chief would get it all sorted. He would probably even let her go home and lie down for a bit, after she gave her statement.

Mindful of the brown smears, she picked her way to

the phone and lifted the handset.

Dead.

She crossed the blood path to another desk, picked up that handset. Nothing. Her fingers shaking, Berta checked that the cord of the phone was plugged into both the wall and the receiver. The phones looked fine.

There was a tiny scraping sound from the direction of the jail cells. Berta jumped. "Hello?" she called, taking a step closer. She forgot to avoid stepping on the rust-colored smears. "Who's back there?" she demanded in her best grandma voice.

There was a soft, low moan, and suddenly Berta's head filled with a whole scene, like from the television: The officers had arrested a violent criminal, who'd beaten up the watch II and locked them in the cell, then ran away, slitting Junie's throat on the way out so she wouldn't call for help. That had to be what had happened. It was almost a relief to have a framework, even if it meant poor Junie was dead.

Berta rushed toward the cells, her hands already thrust out to pull open the door. Her face lined up with the little window, she looked inside, and—

Huh. There was a pileup.

That was how Berta's brain interpreted it, anyway. A whole pile of bodies was wedged into the small space between the row of cells and the wall. As a diehard Bears fan, for the first, dazed moment, Berta saw only the results of some sort of amateur football game.

Then she registered the chief's dead eyes, staring at her from the very top of the pile. There was a missing strip of skin from his double chin, with brown stains all around it.

Berta screamed, the sound seeming to echo forever in the empty bullpen, but she couldn't tear her eyes away. Then, below the chief, at the very bottom of the pile of corpses, a bloodstained hand began to move.

Berta fainted dead away.

Chapter 3

Until she'd been more or less coerced into working for the anti-shade task force, Lindy had never been in an FBI building . . . but she was pretty sure they weren't supposed to look like this.

The slightly run-down structure was only a few blocks from the Chicago FBI headquarters, and it had once been home to several private businesses. The government now owned the building, but at the moment the BPI occupied only one suite. No one was quite sure what to do with the rest of the space, at least until it was determined just how big a threat the shades of Chicago were going to be. There had been talk of expanding their personnel after Hector's people raided the building, but that budget eventually went to opening up new branches of the BPI on the West Coast, and the Chicago pod got a small pittance for new door locks.

In the end, the Chicago BPI, which consisted of six agents, one office manager, and what seemed like a rotating door of federally funded temps, continued to work in a space that had been designed for a hundred, inside a building that should have been filled with double that.

After the incident with Hector, which left six of the loaned-out FBI agents dead, Alex's team had instinctively closed ranks—literally. One small office had been set aside for the special agent in charge, but everyone else worked with their desks huddled together in the improvised bullpen, surrounded by yards and yards of empty space. Lindy often wondered how long it would take before any of them began to relax in this building that was supposed to be their stronghold.

She was always the first one in the door—shades rarely needed to sleep, and Lindy liked to get into the building before the sun rose, so she could check the security with her shade powers intact. She finished her prowl around the empty building, and, thinking of her conversation with Bartell, dutifully went to her desk to work on her paperwork, telling herself that she could be a team player.

A little before seven, she felt it—the gradual death of her body, like the turning of a knob on a gas fireplace until the flames are *almost* extinguished. Unlike some of her kind, Lindy believed that becoming a shade was a biological condition, the result of a particularly strange but by no means supernatural virus. But there were two moments in every day when, just for a few minutes, she wondered if magic were real after all. Because feeling your body first extinguish and then flare to life, every day, never felt natural.

Dulled and diminished, Lindy tried to keep her focus on the reports, and on listening for her coworkers. At seven-thirty, she heard the low, sensible heels of the office manager, Sarah Greer.

"Good morning, Sarah," she said as the door opened.

"Good morning, Miss Frederick," she said carefully, shrugging out of her coat. No matter how many times Lindy asked, most of the BPI staff insisted on calling her "Miss Frederick."

"I started the coffee for you," Lindy offered.

"Thank you, Miss Frederick." The office manager retrieved a mug of caffeine from the break room and settled in at her desk, her body unconsciously turned just a little sideways, to keep Lindy in her peripheral vision.

A few minutes ticked by, while an uncomfortable silence settled around them. Eventually Sarah raked a hand through her neat bob. "He should be here by eight," she announced.

Lindy smiled. It was seven thirty-five. "I know."

After two weeks in the hospital, and another ten days

testifying and taking meetings in Washington, Special Agent in Charge Alex McKenna was finally returning to work.

A few minutes later, another set of heels on the lobby floor: That would be Agent Jill Hadley, the youngest member of the BPI's Chicago pod. Hadley swung the door open, wearing her black leather boots with a three-inch square heel, and a spotless, if drab, suit. Hadley's clothes always seemed designed for invisibility, but her one big vanity was her long red hair. It was grown out to her waist, although she kept it in a tight French braid most days. Lindy liked her more for the hair, which was not in line with the functional styles favored by the female FBI agents Lindy had met. "Eight o'clock, right?" Hadley said to Sarah, by way of greeting. Sarah nodded.

Right behind her, the interior door swung open again, and Lindy knew without looking that it would be Agent Ruiz, the only one of them who wore sneakers to work. Ruiz wore a dress shirt and jacket over nice jeans, and although everything he wore smelled clean, he always looked like he'd just dragged himself out of bed, patted his hair down, and magically appeared at the office.

"Good morning, Agent Ruiz," Sarah said smartly. "How was your weekend?"

Ruiz just grunted at her. "What time is he coming?" he asked in his gruff, ex-smoker's voice.

"Eight," Sarah and Hadley said at the same time.

Bartell arrived a few minutes later, although he simply nodded his good morning to everyone, Lindy included. Finally, at seven fifty-nine, Lindy heard Alex McKenna's shoes crossing the lobby floor. To her surprise, she felt a flurry of sensation in her stomach, and realized that it was nerves. She was *nervous*. How quaint.

Then the door swung open, and without being told, every member of the Chicago BPI pod, Lindy included, stood up and applauded.

Special Agent Alex McKenna had once been very good-looking in a clean-cut, captain of the football team kind of way. When the BPI and FBI had raided Hector's lair, though, Lindy's psychotic twin brother had taken a blade to Alex's face and shoulder. He wasn't trying to kill Alex so much as distract Lindy in order to escape, but the agent in charge had still come very close to bleeding out. Lindy had saved Alex's life with a huge infusion of shade saliva, but the diagonal scar that started near his right eye, bumped over his lips, and ended near his jawline was still wide and angry-looking, puckering as his face broke into a smile. The right eye had been sliced too, along the cornea, but the doctors had been able to save it, and he wasn't even wearing the patch anymore.

When Lindy met Alex, his hair had been just this side of shaggy, but the doctors had needed to shave part of it away to stitch up his scalp. Sometime since then, Alex had shorn everything else off to match, leaving a spiky buzz cut. Only a month after she had first met him, Alex McKenna looked like a completely different person from the man who'd appeared in her office in Cincinnati to "recruit" her.

As the clapping went on, Alex's eyes met hers, a small smile playing on his broken lips, and Lindy felt the butterflies in her stomach dissolve. He wasn't upset with her.

He lifted a hand to cut off the applause. "I don't know why you guys are so happy," he said with a lopsided grin. Lindy suspected that it hurt him to smile with both sides of his mouth. "Now that I'm back, you're gonna have to stop screwing around all day."

Everyone snickered. Alex looked around. "Where's Chase?" he said. The question was directed more or less at Sarah, but she nervously looked over her shoulder at Hadley, who glanced at Ruiz, who shrugged. Chase Eddy was Alex's best friend and longtime number two, and nobody wanted to tattle on him.

Finally Lindy spoke up. "He's been working out of the office quite a bit," she said, drawing Alex's gaze. "He didn't tell you?"

"He said he was doing some outreach with local law enforcement agencies in the area, answering questions about shades." After Hector and the ensuing panic, Chase had taken it upon himself to educate every sheriff's office and police department within three hours' driving distance, in the hopes that teaching them to spot the difference between shade attacks and regular human crimes would cut down on the false alarms. It was a good idea, although Lindy privately thought the timing was poor. With Alex gone for so long, it had seemed like a strange time for his second-in-command to go on the road. "I thought he'd be back by now, though," Alex went on. He looked concerned, and though Lindy had little experience with interpersonal human relationships, even she knew it was unlike Chase to miss Alex's return. "Has anyone talked to him?"

They all exchanged looks again. No one wanted to tell Alex that Chase had pretty much left them to their own devices for most of his absence. Lindy hadn't actually laid eyes on him in over two weeks. Alex opened his mouth to say something else, but was interrupted by a teasing voice from the doorway.

"Jeez, make one little stop for donuts and the boss jumps down your throat."

Alex turned around, revealing Chase Eddy leaning in the doorway with a large pink bakery box. He set it down on Sarah's desk. "Hey, brother," Chase said, opening his arms to embrace Alex. "You look good. Definitely more handsome than before."

Alex hugged him, then stepped back to hold Chase at arm's length. "You, on the other hand, look like shit."

Lindy frowned. It was true. Chase was pale, and he had thumbprint-sized dark marks under each eye from lack of sleep. The flu, maybe? She wanted to check his scent, but during the day, she'd need to get a *lot* closer. Now wasn't really the time.

"Dig in, everyone," Chase said, popping open the bakery box. Ruiz, Sarah, and Hadley all stood.

"Chase!" Alex gave his best friend an injured look. "You didn't bring anything for Lindy?"

Everyone stopped moving, and the room went dead silent. Maybe she was being paranoid, but Lindy thought she saw Chase swallow hard.

Then, at almost the exact same moment, every single one of them burst into laughter. Chase doubled up with it, and even grumpy Ruiz let out a hoarse guffaw.

To her shock, Lindy felt actual human tears prick her eyes. Tears of relief.

Maybe it was going to be okay.

Chapter 4

Alex had actually been worried about this moment, about seeing Chase, and especially Lindy. Chase had been unusually bad about returning his calls and texts over the last few weeks, and he'd only stopped by the hospital once, for a few seconds. Alex suspected his friend had found a new girl, but it wasn't like him to let that come between them.

And then there was Lindy. *She* always returned his calls and texts, and was happy to talk about anything related to the office or what she was doing at work. But whenever Alex brought up that strange moment in the hospital, when he could have sworn he heard Lindy's voice inside his head, she shut down the conversation, insisting it was just his drug-fueled imagination.

So when everyone started laughing, and Chase clapped him on the back, Alex nearly sagged with relief. Donut in hand, he extricated himself from the group and headed back to his office. He had to pass Lindy's desk on the way. "Can we talk?" Alex said in a low voice.

She nodded and stood up, her face carefully blank. Physically, Lindy was the opposite of what he once expected a shade to look like. She was blond, curvy, and soft-looking, with an undertone of sexiness that she could play up or down with the right makeup and clothes. Today she had on a light blue sweater set and dressy black pants. She reminded Alex more of the elementary school teacher every little boy crushes on than a bloodsucking creature of the night.

Alex motioned to the visitor chair, which still had a plastic tag attached to one leg. They'd barely had a chance to move into this office before Hector's people had attacked it. "How was your trip?" Lindy asked, her voice studiously casual. "Did they make any decisions?"

He couldn't blame her for asking. As far as they knew, Lindy was the only outed shade in the country who wasn't locked up behind bars. Of course she had a stake—no pun intended—in Congress's debate about shade rights.

But he shook his head. "Everyone is too afraid that declaring shades inhuman will piss them off. Now that they've seen what Hector can do, they're scared of the resulting confrontation. At the same time, many people think declaring shades illegal is the only way to *stop* people like Hector." He sighed. "My guess is that they'll keep stalling until we get more intel on how shades are organized, and how we can fight them. I don't suppose there's anything you'd care to share on that?"

She hesitated for a long moment, and then shook her head.

"Lindy?" He pushed.

"The organization. . . . No. I've been out of that loop for a *long* time. As for the other problem . . ." She winced. "Hector actually may have given me an idea about a way to fight shades, but I hate to take his word for it. I need to think about it a little more, maybe do some testing. And there are some legal complications. It's honestly probably better if you don't know yet."

Alex leaned back in his chair, studying her. Lindy had signed on with them, Alex suspected, mostly because he'd dangled the right carrot: her brother. She wanted to stop him from killing innocents, and was willing to more or less sign a deal with the devil to do it.

It was difficult to figure out how loyal Lindy would be to the BPI, but it was even harder to determine how loyal she was to shades. Fighting Hector was one thing, but in the short time since he'd recruited Lindy, many states had made it illegal to drink blood—which was basically the same thing as criminalizing shades. That put a lot of Lindy's kind in jeopardy. Could he still trust her not to hold back crucial information, if that information might hurt her people? Did she even think of them as "her people"?

Alex had no idea. A month ago, so many BPI agents had been killed that adding a shade to the Chicago pod had seemed like a brilliant, if risky, idea. What better way to figure out how the shades thought than by bringing one into the fold? Alex didn't regret the decision, exactly, but he'd assumed that the captured shade, Ambrose, would give him the name of some average, low-level shade. Instead he'd gotten Lindy, who was not only Hector's twin, but obscenely powerful. So now Alex was in bed—professionally speaking—with a vampire who was obviously stronger than he'd ever dreamed.

And she wanted to keep secrets from him.

He knew what Chase would say—that Lindy was too dangerous, that they needed to start treating her as a hostile witness rather than a teammate. It wasn't anything personal; Chase was just cautious like that.

Lindy was looking calmly back at him, her hands folded carefully in her lap. She could have just lied to him, Alex realized, or mesmerized him to stop asking questions. She *wanted* to trust him, just as he wanted to trust her.

Finally, Alex bobbed his head. "Fine. For now. But I'd like an update soon. Meanwhile, how are we on exposure? Who knows about you?"

"Everyone in this building," she said matter-of-factly. "Agent Palmer. And Noelle, of course." She held up her wrist so Alex could see the bracelet.

Palmer was the official liaison between the Bureau and its weird little offshoot that dealt with vampires. Alex had called him personally from the hospital, and convinced him not to tell anyone about Lindy. Palmer hadn't liked it, but he was old-school Bureau, and for once Alex wasn't above leaning on his mother's reputation. "What about the FBI agents who were with us at the raid?" Alex asked. "They must have seen you in action."

Lindy studied her nails. "They don't remember that part," she said airily. "Neither do the kids we rescued."

Alex suppressed a smile. She'd mesmerized them, but he couldn't really blame her for that, either. "Have you heard anything from Hector?"

She shook her head. "He's gone to ground. I can't even feel his location anymore, which means he's either left Chicago, or he's figured out that a complete transfusion will block me from finding him. Either way, I can't talk to him." She looked like she didn't know if this was a good or a bad thing. She hesitated for a second, and then asked, "Did you go see Ambrose while you were in DC?"

Alex shrugged. "I tried. He just stared at the wall and sang. For two hours."

She considered that for a second. "What song?"

"Killer Queen." He sang a few bars of the chorus. "She's a Killer Queeeeeeeen / Gunpowder, guillotine / Dynamite with a laser beam."

Lindy sighed. "Yeah, that sounds about right."

Alex was about to ask what she meant by that, but over her shoulder he saw Sarah Greer leaning out of the break room, speaking urgently to the others. Hadley and Chase got to their feet and hurried toward her. Ruiz stood more slowly and lumbered after them. "Something's going on," Alex said.

He and Lindy had just stood up when Chase rushed out of the break room, poking his head into Alex's office.

"There's been a multiple murder," Chase said urgently. "I think they're gonna—"

Just then, the desk phones began to ring. Then Alex's cell phone. And Chase's cell phone. Alex met his friend's troubled gaze.

This was going to be bad.

~

While Alex talked on the phone, the others crowded around the television in the break room, fixed on the news. Lindy listened in on Alex's call for a bit, but when it was obvious that Deputy Director Harding was sending their team to Switch Creek, she tuned it out and concentrated on the newscast.

Twelve people—twelve *humans*—had been attacked at a village police station only twenty-five miles north of here. Lindy listened in horror as the anchor explained that eleven of them were dead, mostly police officers. The news anchor couldn't confirm the cause of death yet, but claimed that the victims had been drained of blood.

Then the newscaster—a handsome man of about fifty—touched his ear bud suddenly, his eyes sliding sideways with a look of concentration. He straightened up and spoke into the camera. "We are now being told by state police that the alleged shade attack may have been triggered by an arrest made last night by a Switch Creek police officer. It seems that this officer charged a currently unidentified young man with consumption of blood, which as you know became a crime in the state of Illinois only a few weeks ago. We have no information about whether the young man in question escaped with the attackers or was among the dead."

The news cut to commercial. Lindy looked at Alex, whose brow was furrowed. The others seemed confused as well. It was Ruiz who said, "Why the hell didn't they call us last night? Someone arrests shades half an hour away and we don't get so much as a notification?"

"Sarah?" Alex asked. "Any messages, anything we missed?"

She shook her head. "Even if SCPD didn't have contact info for you guys, calling the office after hours would have routed them to the FBI switchboard, and they could have gotten a hold of any of us."

"All right. I'd like you to check with the switchboard, make sure nobody dropped the ball on our side of things." Lindy could guess what he was worried about—that the Switch Creek police had called them for help, and it had gotten lost in the tremendous flow of false alarms they waded through each day.

The newscaster came back on, repeated the same information again, and promised to inform viewers of any new developments. Ruiz reached up and flicked the switch to another network channel. And another. And another. Each one showed a similar shot of the exterior of the Switch Creek police building. Everyone had interrupted their morning coverage for this story, although no one seemed to have any more details.

"Shit. They woke the bear. Again," Ruiz muttered under his breath. He remembered himself and shot a look over his shoulder at Lindy, but she just nodded. He was right.

After the revelation that vampires, or at least vampire-like creatures, did indeed exist, the public had spent a few weeks panicking and debating, and then they'd all sort of . . . moved on. For months, no other shades were

discovered, and the one shade in captivity, Ambrose, began to seem to the public like a freak accident, a singular
medical irregularity. Lindy, who had spent centuries fret-
ting about public discovery, was astonished at humans'
capacity for apathy. No, not apathy—willful ignorance.
They didn't want to deal with the existence of vampires,
so they'd collectively put their heads down and pushed
on.

Then her brother had spent the summer kidnapping
teenagers in Illinois, and people began to look up from
their iPhones and recognize that shades were actually
a threat, and a terrifying one. In the last two weeks it
had begun to calm down again, but . . . Ruiz was right. If
this was a shade attack—and Lindy had to admit that it
seemed likely, even after all the false alarms of the last few
weeks—this would rouse public outrage, again.

Alex was walking toward the break room door, still
talking on the phone. "Yes, Deputy Director. I will. Are
you—right. Yes, ma'am. . . . I don't know." Alex met her
eyes, and she knew exactly what he was thinking. Hector.
Had her brother orchestrated this? It seemed a little
flashy for him . . . but then again, this had happened in
the vicinity of where he knew she was living. What were
the odds that a shade incident this close wasn't related
to her brother in some way? She shook her head. *I don't
know.*

He hung up and pushed out a breath. "All right, guys, this is ours. What's left of Switch Creek PD is stepping back. The state police are at the scene now, but Deputy Director Harding wants us to take over. She's calling Gil's boss to have him send our forensic team."

They all nodded. Lindy knew from their last case that although the BPI was still way too small to have their own dedicated forensics division, as a splinter of the FBI they had access to Bureau resources—which were probably far more sophisticated than the state police's. She wondered how the state troopers would feel about that, but if Alex wasn't worried, she wasn't either.

"There is one survivor: Amanda Dylan, a twenty-four-year-old patrol officer who just finished her maternity leave. She's in critical condition at Lake Forest Hospital. Hadley, Ruiz, Chase, Lindy, you're with me," Alex went on. "Hadley, do you still have contacts in the area?"

Surprised, Lindy watched the young agent flinch, then give a reluctant nod. "Yes, sir."

"Good. Do—" His phone audibly buzzed, and he stopped talking long enough to read a text. Then he looked up. "Okay. That was from Sergeant Faraday of the Illinois State Police. The young man who was arrested last night is named Aidan Kerns. He was not among the bodies, and is presumed missing."

"Was he working with the attackers?" Chase asked, in his level voice.

"We don't know yet."

"*Kim* Faraday?" Hadley said, her brow furrowed.

"That's right. You know him?"

"I think so. He was at Lake Forest High while I was at Deerfield."

Alex nodded. "Okay. When we get up there, I want you to liaise with him. Work together, make sure the state police stays happy about us marking their territory. I'll clear the arrangement with Harding."

Hadley didn't look very pleased with the assignment, Lindy saw, but she just gave Alex a curt nod. Then the SAC added, "The two of you can go to the hospital and try to interview the survivor. It would be good to have the state police along for that one, make sure we're not stepping on toes more than necessary." Hadley looked a little pacified.

Alex looked at the rest of them. "Lindy and I will take the sedan and head straight to the crime scene. She may see something we would miss, and she can confirm whether the killings were really shades. Hadley, ride with us; you can meet Faraday there. Chase, you and Ruiz take the SUV and go talk to Mary Holbrook, the chief of police's wife. See what you can find out about the arrest from her." Chase's eyes flicked between Alex and Lindy, and for a moment it actually looked like he might protest. But then the other agent just nodded and turned to get keys from Sarah's desk.

"What about me?" Bartell asked the SAC.

"For right now, I want you here. We can't just shutter the windows and hope no other shades kill anyone while we're looking into this," Alex replied. "There could be reprisals or copycat killings, and you'll be fielding calls from the media as well. I'll call Gil and have him send over more floaters."

There was a groan from the general direction of where Ruiz, Hadley, and Chase were lining up by the door. No one liked the floaters, Lindy knew, because they didn't have the context to know what they were doing, and few of them stuck around long enough to figure it out. Lindy understood then that this was part of why Alex had chosen Bartell to hang back. People tended to listen to their elders, and quiet, patient Bartell would be able to herd the floaters into some sort of order while they were gone. He was someone you just naturally took seriously.

As she walked past him to go to the car, Bartell reached out and lightly touched her arm. "Good luck, Miss Frederick," he said quietly. "And please remember our conversation."

For a moment she was irritated, but she could see the worry in his eyes, and she knew it wasn't just for her. They needed to be able to act as a team—and that was going to be hard enough, since they'd spent the last few weeks scattered around. She gave him a nod and followed Alex out the back door to the cars.

Chapter 5

She had been pacing for hours in the small room: back and forth, back and forth; her sneakers scuffing hard on the concrete floor. She wasn't the type to yell at her people, he knew, but she was frustrated and angry, and Sloane couldn't really blame her.

He waited her out, sitting in one of the portable camp chairs with his feet up on a plastic tub. They had only been in the bunker for a few weeks, and if things worked out the way she wanted, they wouldn't be there long.

Eventually, the sun rose, and her steps began to flag. "You need to rest," Sloane said quietly. He didn't want to nag her, but couldn't help adding, "You know you can't stay awake all day yet."

She bared her teeth at him. "I'm fine."

Sloane held his tongue. She did two more circuits of the bunker and then, abruptly, the energy seeped out of her. Her shoulders slumped, and she came over to sit in the chair next to his.

"You're right; I know you're right," she muttered. "I just can't believe how fast that went to hell."

Sloane tilted his head in concession. He'd been on thousands of similar missions over his long life, but that had been a clusterfuck of the highest order.

It hadn't been *her* fault, though.

He glanced to the far end of the bunker, where two male figures were laid out on inflatable mattresses. Cooper was too new to stay awake for any part of the day, even with the influx of blood, and of course the boy wouldn't awaken until sunset. They had time to figure out their next move.

Or at least, he hoped they did. There was a small television in the corner, and they'd had the news on while she paced. The new Bureau of Preternatural Investigations was getting involved, which was not good. They had nearly taken down bloody *Hector*; Sloane didn't want to be anywhere near their radar.

"We should leave," he said. "Tonight, if possible. To-morrow night, if we're taking the boy with us."

She bit her lip. "I haven't decided yet."

He wanted to press his argument, but her eyelids were dragging, and Sloane couldn't help a wave of concern for her. "Get some sleep, Rags," he said. "I'm going to lie down for a few hours myself." He meant it literally: at his age, he didn't really need the sleep, but he wanted a little time to think. And if it encouraged her to rest . . .

She was wavering. Sloane rested a hand gently on her shoulder. She didn't typically like to be touched, but this time she covered his hand with hers and squeezed. "Okay," she conceded. "But I need you to run an errand this afternoon."

~

It was a sunny, crisp fall day, so Lindy pulled a baseball cap and sunglasses out of her bag and put them on. After monitoring Ambrose, the first captured shade, the public knew that some shades could stay awake during the day—but they had no idea that the older ones were also capable of going out in the sun, as long as they didn't linger in direct sunlight. Cars could be hard, with all the windows, but Alex had gotten the two BPI vehicles fitted with smoked, bulletproof glass, which she infinitely appreciated.

Lindy hadn't actually been in a car while Alex was driving before this, but within two minutes of leaving the BPI building she understood why Chase usually took the wheel. Alex swooped through the Chicago traffic with the siren and lights screaming, like they were in an action movie pursuing Jason Bourne. Even during the day,

Lindy could survive most injuries, but she found herself gripping the door handle and squeezing her eyes shut, grateful that she no longer felt actual nausea. Both Alex and Hadley, who sat silently in the backseat, seemed as calm and relaxed as if they were watching television at home.

"How far away is this town?" Lindy asked Alex.

"Thirty miles, and technically I think it's a village. Switch Creek is one of the wealthy northern suburbs of Chicago. It's where investment bankers park their families, away from the dangers of the city." He rolled his eyes. "Or where rich white people go to avoid minorities and the homeless, depending on who you ask."

Lindy half-turned in her seat so she could see Hadley, who was focused on her cell phone. If she was offended by the characterization, it didn't show. "And you're from there?"

She looked up from her phone, hesitating for just a second, like she'd been caught in a lie. "Near there, yes."

Lindy was going to ask her another question, but the young woman was looking at Alex in the rearview mirror. "Boss, I've been checking Facebook. Several people in Switch Creek posted videos of the arrest last night. It's going viral."

"What's on the videos?"

"They're all basically the same. We see a uniformed officer standing opposite a man with a bleeding nose. The man says the cop hit him," Hadley said. "Then he licks blood off his own arm."

"Can I see?" Lindy said quickly, afraid that Alex was going to try to watch the video and drive like a maniac at the same time.

With only the slightest air of reluctance, Hadley passed Lindy an iPhone in a black tactical case. Lindy played the clip, which was less than a minute long. "What's happening?" Alex asked, trying to see over her shoulder.

Lindy leaned toward the window, tilting the phone so he couldn't see. "Watch the road. And hang on a second." Lindy played the video again, holding the screen an inch from her face. Then she shook her head and told Alex about the guy licking the blood off his arm.

"Can you tell if he's a shade?"

"The video's pretty dark, and it's not a great angle," Lindy replied, handing the phone back to Agent Hadley, "but I'm ninety percent sure there's no stimulation response." Shades in the presence of open blood almost always "vamped out," an automatic reaction in which every part of the eye turned blood red. The older you were, the better you could control it. But Aidan would have to be a young vampire. "I don't think he plays for my team," Lindy concluded.

"Huh. So technically, he broke the new anti-shade law, but there's no indication he's really a shade."

"Exactly."

"What time was the video posted?" Alex asked, looking at Hadley in the rearview mirror.

She checked the screen again. "Eleven-oh-eight last night. So why didn't the news pick this up?"

"Because someone made sure they wouldn't," Alex said grimly.

Chapter 6

One of the best things about working for the Bureau, in Jill Hadley's opinion, was the anonymity that came with being one of "them." Unlike regular police departments, which varied by population and location, the Bureau *wanted* their agents to be as cookie-cutter as possible. Hadley knew a couple of people from the academy who chafed against this attitude, but she saw her sameness as a shield, a convenient surface that she could hide behind. No, not hide behind—relax behind. She could let her guard down because someone else had installed premade armor over her instead. And now, her precious outer coating was going to dissolve.

She had always known that one of the reasons she was kept in the Chicago area, first by the Bureau, and now the BPI, was because she had value as a local. She'd gone to Northwestern; she knew Chicagoland. Ordinarily she didn't mind being the resident Chicago expert, but she'd never imagined she'd be sent back home to the suburbs on a case. The whole idea was ridiculous, really. Deerfield, and the cluster of villages around it, including Switch Creek, Lake Forest, and a few others, were so safe, so all-American white suburbia, that they were actually the inspiration for John Hughes's '80s high school comedies. These upper-middle-class mini-towns weren't just the suburbs, they were what people thought about when they thought of suburbs. And Jill Hadley had secrets there.

As Special Agent McKenna navigated the traffic on I-90 out of Chicago, Hadley tried to push these thoughts out of her mind, instead using her laptop to look through the little information she could find on Aidan Kerns. They were nearly the same age, but he'd gone to school in Switch Creek, not Deerfield, and he hadn't played in any of the sports that competed with her school. He didn't have a social media presence—not even a Facebook page—and had never been arrested or owned property. His driver's license photo showed a pale young man with a crisp dress shirt and a startled expression. He could be anybody.

"Oh, wow," came Agent McKenna's voice from the front seat. Hadley looked up to see her boss staring out the window. They were in Switch Creek, and even on the streets leading into town, the gorgeous oaks were displaying a full burst of autumn color. The explosion of oranges and reds seemed to shine out of the trees, thanks to the sun peeking through them.

"I bet you were a city kid," Lindy said, sounding amused.

"We had field trips in DC," McKenna said, a little defensive. "I've just never seen fall colors like this."

They were already entering the "downtown" district, which resembled, more than anything, the campus of a small but well-funded private college. The buildings were all done in matching sand-colored brick, set out carefully in landscaped connecting rows that would never be associated with the term *strip mall,* though they served the same function. These commercial properties were filled with national high-end stores—Elizabeth Arden, Nordstrom—and the kind of expensive restaurants that would describe their menu items as "artisanal." Despite the local tragedy, there were plenty of people out and about, arms filled with shopping bags or pushing strollers. Most of them had anxious and worried expressions, and Hadley suspected they were trying to get errands done so they could be off the streets well before dark. This was not a community that would adapt well to being threatened by vampires.

"Everything's so clean," Alex observed, craning his head to look out the front window. "And there are no homeless people."

"And everyone is white," Lindy added, her tone neutral. She was right, of course—there were very few minority faces on the street, although Hadley knew from experience that it wasn't a matter of racism, at least not in the traditional sense. The people who lived in these villages cared about money, safety, and prestige, but they also wanted to be *seen* as inclusive and welcoming, which meant there was a certain cachet in having the occasional rich Indian American or African American family move into one of the local mansions. Being able to brag about diversity would be a feather in their cap—at least, up to a point.

"Still," McKenna said in a quiet voice. "It *is* beautiful."

Hadley sighed, her heart sinking. She was back, if not in her own suburb, in a nearly identical one not ten miles away. "Yeah. It is."

~

The police station was a pretty brick building two blocks from the town square, down a side street that served as an alley to other public buildings. Alex was guessing people here wanted to feel like the cops were nearby, but not right on top of them.

The state police had blocked off the street with sawhorses, setting up yellow crime scene tape around the lawn. Despite their efforts, the whole area was still swarming with people trying to press closer. Most of them were media, judging by all the reporters primping in the side mirrors of their news vans, but there was also a whole contingent of locals: well-dressed men and women, often with kids in strollers, leaning over the tape to yell questions about their loved ones or criticize the way vampires had ruined the town. Some of it was ugly, and Alex kept an eye on Lindy as they slammed the doors of the sedan. If she was bothered by the anti-shade sentiment, however, it didn't show.

The lot was packed with news vans and angry people, so Alex left the sedan on the street, flashing his badge to the state trooper who hurried over to yell at him. He gestured at Hadley and Lindy, who held up a badge and a consultant's ID, respectively. The trooper read them carefully and then, looking a little disappointed, he let the three of them duck under the crime scene tape. Alex moved quickly up the stairs to the entrance. Lindy was wearing a baseball cap and sunglasses, but the autumn sunshine was still filtering through the trees, and he didn't want to expose her to the sun any longer than necessary.

Once he was past the crowd and taking a good look, he was surprised by the quality of the police department building. It could only be a few years old, for one thing, and although the size was modest, everything seemed chosen to look good as well as function—which was at odds with most of the government buildings Alex had been inside.

They went through the outer door into the breezeway, where a middle-aged, sturdy-looking woman stood up from the folding chair where she'd been waiting. Her makeup had run down into her collar from crying, but she was calm, her red-rimmed eyes sharp and competent. She stuck out a hand to Alex. "I'm Berta Hauptmann," she blurted. "I'm the office manager who found the bodies. State police asked me to wait for you."

Alex read her nervousness and the way her eyes darted toward the exit, and took her hand in both of his. "Thank you so much for sticking around for us, Berta," he said solemnly. "I'm sure this must be so difficult for you. I'm Special Agent in Charge Alex McKenna, and these are my colleagues Special Agent Hadley and Rosalind Frederick."

Hadley stepped forward to shake hands dutifully. Lindy, for her part, was already looking past Berta into the room beyond, her nostrils flaring. Alex pulled gloves and booties from a bag in his pocket. Hadley did the same, and Alex handed an extra set to Lindy. The last thing they needed was anyone picking up Lindy's DNA or fingerprints. Assuming she had any.

"Have they moved the bodies yet?" Alex asked the office manager while they dressed.

"They took Junie away, because she was just inside the door and the photographers were trying to get pictures of her," she told him. "And we had to take some of the . . . bodies . . . out of the jail cells in order to get to Officer Dylan, the survivor." She rubbed nervously at her hands, which were clean, but the skin looked raw from vigorous scrubbing. She had probably needed to clean blood from her hands. "But the rest of them are still back there." Berta gave them a shaky smile. "That's why I'm waiting out here. Not very brave of me."

"You're doing great," Alex assured her. He meant it: The woman had discovered the dead bodies of most of her coworkers, the same people she talked, laughed, ate, and argued with every day. They lived in a place that was supposed to be safe, and the police department should have been the safest of all. The fact that Berta was still walking and talking, trying to help, was impressive. "Do you think you'd be able to walk us through the scene as you found it?"

She swallowed hard, shifting from one foot to the other. Alex held out his elbow in an old-fashioned gesture. That made her smile just a little, and she took his arm. "Okay," she said, almost to herself. "One more time."

They went through the inner door, with Lindy in the

lead, looking distracted and worried. Alex let Berta Hauptmann ramble through her story, half-listening, with the rest of his attention focused on Lindy. Hadley was as quiet as ever, but her sharp eyes were flicking around the room, observing everything in her guarded way. Lindy looked at the desk where the dispatcher must have lain for just a moment, and then she lifted her head and hurried toward to the back of the room, turning right without needing directions.

"That's the bullpen," Berta explained to Alex as the three of them trailed after Lindy. "Has she been here before?"

"I'm not sure," Alex replied. "What were you saying about slipping on the blood?"

The bullpen was a single large room with desks, and two doors against the back wall, one of which was open. It looked like the room beyond had vomited out bodies. Bloodied corpses were strewn across the floor, reminding Alex of someone digging for something in a closet, tossing discarded items over their shoulder. Alex winced. He understood why they'd needed to move the bodies to extract the survivor, but the forensics team was going to be incensed when they arrived.

Speaking of irritating the crime scene people, there were several state police milling around, taking photos and murmuring into handheld voice recorders. Alex was annoyed: They were supposed to have locked down the building and waited outside for the FBI forensics team. Why were they investigating?

"Who's the officer in charge back here?" he asked Berta in a low voice.

Her lips pursed disapprovingly as she pointed to a heavyset man squatting next to one of the corpses. There was a lean Asian man standing beside him, hands in his pockets. "Lieutenant Dennis Lassner."

Alex gave her a conspiratorial smile. "I take it you've worked with him before?"

She snorted. "He thinks he's Columbo. He was the only one who fought against calling you guys in."

The last thing Alex needed was a territorial dispute, especially from a guy who looked like he'd read a book called *How to Look Like a Cop* and followed the instructions diligently. Lassner was in his late forties, with a trim haircut, handlebar mustache, and a small potbelly hanging over his belt. He was already starting to rise as they walked in, but Lindy ignored him and went straight toward the door to the jail cells.

Lassner stood up fast, his knees audibly cracking as he blocked Lindy's way. "Who the hell are you?" he demanded.

She just glanced over her shoulder, raising an eyebrow. Alex stepped up. "She's with me," he said easily. He strode over to Lassner, hand extended. "Alex McKenna, Special Agent in Charge."

Lindy took the opportunity to circle around him toward the bodies. The state cop scowled, but took Alex's hand. "They gonna turn?" He demanded.

"Excuse me?"

The older man made an impatient noise, flapping a hand at the bodies. "Are these people going to turn into vampires?"

Alex glanced over Lassner's shoulder at Lindy, who glanced down and then shook her head almost imperceptibly. "No," he told Lassner.

The lieutenant relaxed a little. "Well, good, then."

If he hadn't been watching for it, Alex would have probably missed Lindy stiffen just a little. He pushed on. "I'd like you and your people to clear the room, Trooper. The Bureau's forensic people will be here any minute, and they won't appreciate the extra people."

Lassner glowered at him. "We're not finished here."

"Yes," Alex said in a harder tone, stepping forward, "you are. I appreciate the crowd control, but now you need to let us do our jobs."

The Asian man now stepped between them with an apologetic smile. "Hi, I'm Sergeant Faraday. Good to meet you in person."

Alex recognized the interception and let it happen,

turning to introduce Hadley and Lindy with an equal degree of politeness. When the moment of civility reached its conclusion, he turned to Lassner again. "Like I was saying, Lieutenant, I appreciate the care you've taken with the scene, but we're done taking up your time and resources."

Berta, to his surprise, released Alex's arm and stepped forward. "I'll walk you out, Dennis," she said in a nectar-sweet voice. "You can fill me in on how Jennie's volleyball team is doing. I could really use the distraction."

The chubby cop glared at both of them, but he knew he was outplayed. He allowed Berta to take his arm, and whistled at the other two investigators. "Let's roll. Faraday, you're with the feds."

Alex met Hadley's eyes. "Call me when you're done at the hospital." She nodded at him, her face as impassive as ever.

Chapter 7

SWITCH CREEK POLICE STATION
FRIDAY MORNING

After the state cops departed, and Hadley went off with Faraday, Alex was finally able to turn and examine the crime scene properly, stepping into the bullpen and looking at the door on the opposite wall. It led to a small room with three gleaming cells. They weren't the Hilton or anything, but they were probably the nicest jail cells Alex had ever seen. One of the cell doors was stuck in the open position, but all the remaining bodies were piled in front of the cells, not inside.

"They weren't all drained," Lindy said, squatting next to one of the corpses. During much of the pissing contest with the state police, she'd been ghosting around the room, checking the bodies. "Some of them had their necks snapped."

"How many?"

Lindy took another glance around, calculating. "Six drained, I think. I . . . um . . . don't want to get too close."

A look of embarrassment flashed across her face, and Alex realized she was fighting the stimulation response. He knew Lindy had excellent control—he'd seen what it took to make her vamp out—but the smell of this much fresh death would be hard even for her. "We'll get more info from Reyes," he told her, trying to sound reassuring. Jessica Reyes was the FBI pathologist who was attached to any BPI cases. She'd done great work on the Hector kidnappings, and Alex had called earlier that morning to make sure she'd be riding up with the Bureau forensics team.

"Was this really shades?" Alex asked Lindy, half-hoping the answer would be no. If this was another ordinary human crime, it would be someone else's problem.

But she nodded. "Even during the day, the whole room reeks of it. Two of them for sure, possibly three. I could tell them apart better after sunset." She crouched down, examining the body of a young man in his late twenties wearing a SCPD uniform. He was lying on his stomach. She glanced up at Alex. "Can I touch them?"

"Better not, until the crime scene people do their thing."

"All right." Undeterred, she lowered her face nearly to the floor so she could peer at the underside of the kid's hand. She frowned to herself and stood up, sniffing the air as she moved away from the bodies. "Hang on." She stepped carefully away from the bodies, back into the bullpen, and across the room to one of the darkened offices. She stepped all the way in, flicked on the lights, and turned to face the wall with the door. She winced. "Did you know about this?" she asked. "They must have kept it off the news."

Moving carefully around the bodies, Alex went over to join her.

There was a message written on the chief's wall in blood.

THIS IS WHAT HAPPENS.

"No, I didn't know. I'm not sure anyone else has even seen this yet."

"That last body's hand was slashed through the palm," she said. "There's blood on his face, but I think he's the cop who arrested the kid. They cut him and then mesmerized him to write the message. That, or used him as a paintbrush, but the writing is too clear for that. I don't think he was struggling."

"'This is what happens,'" Alex mused. "Has kind of a creepy finality to it. But what does it mean?"

"Could be 'this is what happens when you make shades public,' or 'this is what happens when you arrest one of us.'"

"But then why put it in the chief's office? Why not

somewhere more visible to everyone?"

"That, I don't know."

"Can you tell if the kid they arrested was really a shade?"

She went back across the room and into the open cell, looking around for a minute, then shrugged. "I just smell shade, but I don't know if it was him or the attackers. Again, I could tell you more after dark."

"How much more?" he asked, just out of plain curiosity.

She paused, and Alex could see her thinking through the question. It was probably strange to put into words something that came naturally, like trying to describe how to blink. "Right now, I can smell shade, and fear . . . and human body smells, because those are overpowering," Lindy said finally. "I can pick out a few ordinary scents too, like deodorant and shampoo and cotton, but it's faint, and I couldn't pair it with a person. When I get my strength back after sunset, I could probably tell you how many people were in this room based on their combinations of products and pheromones, assuming more people haven't tracked through here in the meantime. Scents fade, even in a windowless room."

Alex was interested. "The scent combination thing—is that like a fingerprint?"

"Not exactly, no. For example, you and Chase smell

nearly the same, because you spend a lot of time in the same places and trade clothes sometimes."

Alex felt his cheeks redden. "Only because I never remember to keep extra shirts at the office."

She shrugged. "My point is, if you made an effort to switch to Chase's toothpaste and aftershave, you could probably fool me, at least during the day. So it's not the same as a fingerprint, but it's a jumping-off point."

"Like a polygraph," Alex mused. The man closest to him looked familiar, and Alex recognized him from one of the pictures on the wall. He squatted down. "This is the chief of police."

The guy was about sixty, but a lean, strong-looking sixty. He was tan and well kept, with neat fingernails and recently trimmed hair. A man who took care of his appearance. Alex shook his head. Just yesterday, this man had been in charge of the whole town's safety. Now he was lying dead on a cold tile floor with his spinal cord showing through his neck. He smelled like blood and viscera, and Alex stood up to get away from it.

And that was just one body. There were so many others. The last time he'd seen this much gore, it had been caused by the will of a single person. "Could this have been Hector?"

"I don't think so," Lindy answered. "Not because he wouldn't kill so many people at once—he has before—but for Hector it would have to be useful to him in some way."

The phrasing sounded harsh, but Alex understood: over the summer, Lindy's brother had killed a number of teens as a side effect of his experiments with transmutation. "How do we know this isn't useful in some way?" he pointed out. "As a misdirect, maybe?"

"Hector's too arrogant for that. If it was him, he'd want you to know it," she said matter-of-factly. She was staring at the body at her feet, a gangly woman in her early forties, her stomach slightly poofed out from having kids. Like the others, she was bloodless, her eyes staring dully out of her gray waxy face. "Besides, if Hector had done this, it would have been cold, and strategic. This wasn't a chess move, Alex," she said, looking up at him. "This was *angry*. Like someone having a tantrum."

"Hey, kids," called a familiar voice from the front of the building.

"We're back here, Jessica," he yelled back.

"Cool. I gotta unload my stuff. Be with you shortly."

Alex turned back to Lindy, not wanting to lose his train of thought. "You said someone, singular? I thought—"

"Oh, there was more than one shade here, that's for sure, but . . ." Her eyes traveled over the words again, then she looked back through the doorway at the bodies. "This whole raid, that wasn't a mob decision. It was too careful, at least at first. It was one person's plan." She shook her head. "I'm just not sure how it all fits together."

Alex took that in for a moment, then nodded. "But he or she made a point to leave that message in the chief's office. What are they hoping to accomplish? Is this a political thing, like they want us to legalize shades, or are they just telling us to be afraid?"

Lindy turned to stare at him, one eyebrow raised. There was something in her face that startled Alex: an alienness that he'd only glimpsed a few times. "Why would you think the message was for humans?"

Chapter 8

As Hadley walked out to Faraday's unmarked car, she could feel him glancing at her.

"You look really familiar," he said at last. "And yet I feel like I would remember working with a pretty fed before."

Ugh. They got into the car, and she decided to just move the conversation along. "I grew up in Deerfield. Anyway, do you—"

Kim Faraday brightened. "Wait, *Jill* Hadley? I remember you! You were a cheerleader."

"I remember you, too." Kim Faraday had been famous when they were in school—partly because of his own football record, partly because his father had once been an honest-to-goodness Chicago Bear ... and partly because he was one of the few nonwhite kids in the school district. Kim's mother had immigrated to the United State from Vietnam as a little girl.

People were surprised when Kim Faraday didn't follow his father into professional ball, Hadley remembered, but she'd had no idea he became a cop, much less a state cop based near his hometown.

"And if you tell any of my colleagues about the cheerleading, I will rip out your tongue and feed it to my boss's cat," she added in her most pleasant voice.

Faraday grinned. "Fair enough," he said easily. Then the smile faded slowly from his face, and Hadley recognized the look, because it was exactly why she didn't come back here anymore. He was remembering what had happened to her brother. "Oh . . . hey . . ."

"So, which hospital again?" she said abruptly.

One thing you had to say for the suburbs: It didn't take long to get anywhere. Within ten minutes, they were pulling up at the ER. Plenty of news vans had already beat them there—the survivor's name hadn't been released, but it wasn't difficult to figure out which ER was the closest to the police station. Some of the state troopers were busy keeping the reporters at bay, so Hadley let Faraday take the lead. When they got inside, he flashed his badge and his smile at the intake nurses, who called the appropriate doctor out to talk to them.

Dr. Weber was a balding white man in his early sixties, with an air of grim concern that Hadley suspected was just his permanent demeanor. They explained that they were there to see the surviving victim, Amanda Dylan.

"She really shouldn't be seeing anyone," he said, his frown lines deepening. "She lost more than half her blood volume; she's lucky to be alive."

"Is she conscious?" Hadley asked.

"On and off, but—"

"She's a cop," Faraday interrupted him. "Trust me, she's going to want to talk to us. Give her my name."

There was an intensity in his voice that surprised Hadley, and as they followed Weber down a long hall, she glanced at Faraday, who had ceased his small talk. His jaw muscles were tightening, like he was clenching and unclenching his teeth, and then it struck her: Faraday was from Switch Creek, and as a state cop he would occasionally work with the local police.

He knew Amanda Dylan. Goddammit. She'd been so busy obsessing over her own personal drama that she'd missed something obvious. "Were you friends?" she asked him under her breath.

For a second he looked startled, but then the easy smile was back. "Mostly just to say hello," he replied. "She isn't from here, but we have sons who go to the same school, and we would sit together at local briefings sometimes. Her husband is friends with my cousin."

Well, that was the suburbs for you. Hadley was annoyed with herself: not only had she missed Faraday's connection to the victim, she'd made an assumption about him being single and childless based on his lack of a wedding ring, like this was the 1800s.

When they reached Dylan's room, the doctor made them wait in the doorway while he and a nurse approached the bed. Hadley looked at the patient: a petite woman in a blue hospital gown, blankets pulled up to her armpits. She was breathing on her own, but there were IVs in both arms, and a blood pressure monitor was attached to her finger. There were several other machines that Hadley didn't even recognize. Dylan's face was so pale that it looked blue next to the gown. Her eyes were closed, and a thick white bandage was wound around her neck. Gold-tinged blond hair was tied in a messy bun above her head, more to keep the hair out of the way than as a fashion statement.

Dr. Weber went over to the bed and touched her hand. "Officer Dylan," he said in a low, surprisingly soothing voice.

She roused slowly, as though she had to surface from deep, deep water in order to open her eyes. Her gaze wandered around the room for a moment before settling on the doctor. "Where's Jake?" she said, her voice weak and sleepy.

"Your husband went to drop off your daughter with your mother-in-law," the nurse told her. According to the sign on the wall, her name was Shelly. "He'll be back soon."

"Oh . . . okay."

"Do you feel able to speak to the police for a few minutes?" Weber asked, in a tone that suggested he knew he was asking too much and would be happy for her to refuse. "A Sergeant Faraday is here."

Dylan's eyes narrowed with sudden clarity. "*Hell* yes," she whispered.

The doctor turned, waving them forward with another one of his frowns. Hadley was really getting used to them. "Five minutes," he ordered. "Absolutely no more." He practically stomped out of the room, leaving Shelly to wait just outside the door.

Hadley introduced herself and got out her notebook, but Amanda Dylan didn't even wait for the first question. She couldn't move her neck, but her eyes fixed on Faraday.

"Kim," Dylan said in a faint whisper. "There were three."

Faraday smiled at her, and this time it reached his eyes. "Hello to you, too, Amanda. Were they men? Women? What races?"

"White man, late twenties, British accent. White woman, midtwenties. Black man . . . maybe forty. The woman was in charge."

"Did you get any names?"

"No. They didn't use them."

"Did they mesmerize any of you?" Hadley asked. It was important to know how good Dylan's memories were, especially if the case went to trial.

Dylan's eyes went distant for a second. "I think so. . . . I'm missing time."

"What *do* you remember about the attack?" she asked.

"Coming into the station. Putting away my weapon. I decided just to stay and fill out my report while it was fresh. Terry came in with the Kerns kid. Then someone touched my hand. . . ." On the sheet, her fingers twitched.

Shade saliva. Lindy had talked to them about this, and Hadley knew it was as simple as a shade touching their lip or pretending to scratch his nose, getting a little saliva on the finger, and touching the victim. It would be hard for one shade to infect a whole room full of people before someone figured out what was happening, but three shades . . . if they split up and worked the room, it seemed feasible.

"Then I couldn't move," Dylan went on. Her voice began to shake, and her eyes were full of horror. "There was shooting, and they were just mauling people."

"Oh, 'Manda, I'm so sorry," Faraday said, touching her hand. She flinched a little, like the memory of being mesmerized was just too close.

Sympathy was the wrong move. Hadley edged closer.

"Officer Dylan," Hadley began, and the woman's attention snapped to her. "The doctor said they took more than half your blood volume, but the other victims appear to be completely drained. Can you tell me why they let you live?"

"I don't know. She was ... *drinking* me," she whispered. "Like I was a keg of beer. I've never been so scared." The beeping of her heart monitor increased in speed, to a point where Hadley half-expected the nurses to come running. Dylan lifted a hand, and Hadley thought the other woman was going to touch the bandage on her neck. But her fingers came to rest across her chest, in a protective gesture. "Her hand bumped my bra. She felt the pads." Her eyelids fluttered.

Hadley shot Faraday a confused look. "Pads?" she whispered.

"From nursing the baby," he explained, blushing a little. "There are these sticky pads you put in your nursing bra, in case there's leakage. My ex-wife used to go through a bunch of them every day."

"Amanda?" Hadley said in a loud, clear voice. "What happened then?"

"She pulled my shirt back to look. She swore. Then she spat on her hand and touched the bite. I was so scared. . . ." Dylan's eyes drifted closed, as if this last burst of speech had finally undone her. Hadley jumped as one of the machines attached to Dylan began screaming, and then the sound of pounding footsteps came down the hall. Shelly burst in, with Dr. Weber on their heels.

"Hypotension," Shelly barked, checking the machines. "She's coding. We need the crash cart."

"What did I tell you!" Weber shouted at them. To the nurse, he added, "Get them out of here!" Startled, Hadley and Faraday eased toward the back of the room, and out the door.

Chapter 9

Gabriel Ruiz had been expecting the police chief's house to be fairly modest, like most public servants', but the residence they pulled up to was massive, with two-story arches on either side of the double doors that formed the entrance.

"What do you think?" Ruiz said to Chase Eddy as they parked at the curb and approached the building. "Six bedrooms?"

"Mmm."

This was Ruiz's first time working one-on-one with Eddy, and to his surprise, the assistant SAC had turned out to be remarkably quiet. Which was fine by Ruiz. Even Hadley, reserved as she was, would sometimes feel obligated to fill long silences. Riding with Eddy was kind of refreshing.

At the door, they were greeted by an actual maid, a pretty Hispanic woman of about fifty, dressed in black pants and a white button-down top. Her eyes lit up when she saw Ruiz. "*Habla Español?*" she asked, sounding a little desperate.

"*Sí.*" In Spanish, he introduced himself and asked her if Mrs. Holbrook was at home. According to the state police, she had been notified earlier that morning.

"*Sí, ella está,*" said the maid, whose name was Estrella.

After checking with her boss, Estrella led them through several luxurious rooms and into a sunken living room with a cream-colored leather seating area. Ruiz asked if anyone was with Mrs. Holbrook—it was customary for the police to call a friend or clergyman—but Estrella shrugged and told him that no, Mrs. Holbrook hadn't wanted anyone else there. Ruiz and Eddy declined drinks, and after a few minutes, Mary Holbrook stepped silently into the room.

She was younger than her husband, maybe in her mid-forties, petite and trim in an athletic way that suggested she worked hard for it. She wore a burgundy tailored suit with a knee-length skirt. Both the skirt and blazer were wrinkled, and her fancy bun—chignon? Was that the word?—was ruffled. She wore stockings with no shoes. She had been wearing makeup at one point, but now her eyes were red and her face was blotchy, making her look like someone had splashed water on a portrait that was still drying.

"I was just lying down for a moment," she explained. "Kevin did tell me you'd be stopping by, but . . . I suppose I forgot."

She came over to shake their hands, and Ruiz saw the dilated pupils. She'd taken some kind of sedative, but he couldn't really blame her. Her husband and a bunch of his employees had been murdered by vampires.

"Kevin?" Eddy asked politely.

"Sorry, Kevin Stone, Glenn's second-in-command. He worked the day shift yesterday. Glenn did too, of course, but he stayed late because of the festival. Kevin did the notification this morning, as I was leaving for work." She gave them an unhappy smile. "I felt sorry for him, really. I've been a cop's wife for so many years. I knew his script as well as he did." Her voice began to tremble at the end, so Ruiz decided to steer her into safer waters.

"Where do you work?"

"I'm an architect at Pearson Lloyd," she said, in a tone that suggested they'd instantly recognize the name. Eddy nodded, and Ruiz wondered if maybe he did. Architects probably made good money in Chicago; this might explain the enormous house.

"Have you been there long?" Eddy asked.

"Nearly twelve years. But you need to ask me about Glenn. It's all right, I understand."

Ruiz exchanged a glance with Eddy. She might have

been wearing pearls, but she was a cop's wife, all right. "Was there anyone who has a particular grudge against your husband?" Eddy asked.

She nodded in something like approval. "I expected you'd ask that. I've thought of little else, for the last few hours. Switch Creek just isn't really a place where one makes that kind of enemy. Glenn was a beat cop in the city for a few years, before we met, and I could see how you might arrest a drug dealer and he'd take it personally. But here . . ." She shrugged. "There's very little crime at all. Glenn would occasionally get some pushback about a community referendum or who wasn't being accepted at which country club. But certainly nothing you'd kill for. And it's been so quiet." Her eyes filled. "He was always home for dinner."

"What about just people who disliked him? Did he butt heads with anyone?"

It was more or less the same question, phrased a little differently, but Mary Holbrook paused, considering it. "There was a state policeman who didn't like Glenn," she said slowly. "Dennis . . . mmm . . . Glassner or Lassner, something like that." Ruiz made a note. "But I always saw it as more of a professional rivalry." She waved a hand, suddenly eager to backpedal. "I'm sure that's nothing. I never paid him much attention."

"Did you notice anything unusual with Glenn's finances?" Eddy said, in the same casual, gentle voice so she wouldn't take offense. "Money added, money leaving, that kind of thing?"

She stared at them blankly. "I thought . . . why would our finances matter? A vampire killed everyone out of revenge."

"That is still our working theory, ma'am, but we do need to cover all our bases."

She shook her head, looking a little pacified. "Nothing unusual."

They asked her a few more of the standard questions about whether Holbrook had been behaving strangely, or if he'd been working any big cases, but she kept shaking her head. "To be honest, I've been so wrapped up in work and volunteering, I've hardly seen Glenn over the past few weeks." Her voice broke, and the realization that now she would *never* see him again washed over her face.

"What do you know about Terry Anson?" Ruiz asked.

Her face instantly changed, the grief being replaced by a long-nursed irritation. "Oh, *him*. Terry was an asshole, if you'll pardon my language."

In Ruiz's experience, witnesses usually needed to be coaxed into speaking ill of the recently dead. Terry Anson must have *really* been an asshole. "What makes you say that?"

She sighed. "I've known Terry for most of his life. After he flunked out of college, his father begged Glenn to let him join the department. They'd played golf together for years, you see, so Glenn agreed to take Terry on as a favor, at least temporarily. Physically, Terry fit the part wonderfully, but when it came to actual police work, he was lazy, and easily frustrated. When it became clear that Glenn wasn't going to be handing out promotions like Little League participant trophies, Terry all but gave up. He's been phoning it in for years now."

"Why didn't your husband fire him?" Eddy asked.

"Because if Terry Anson had one talent, it was to know the exact fine line between a poor work ethic and a fireable offense." She made a face. "And because the one time that moron *did* show initiative was when the union rep came to visit. Terry would take him out for drinks, show him a good time."

"How did Glenn feel about that?"

"He was frustrated, of course, but in another few years he planned to retire, and Anson would be someone else's problem," she said with a shrug. "Meanwhile, Glenn kept an eye out for anything he could use against him. Terry had started drinking more, I know. Glenn was hoping to catch him drunk on duty, which would be enough to finally get rid of him. But he never got the chance."

Ruiz made a note to ask Jessica Reyes, the pathologist, to rush a blood alcohol test on Terry Anson. If he'd been drunk when he decided to arrest an alleged shade, it could change some things.

"Were you at the festival, ma'am?" Eddy asked.

She blinked hard, looking surprised. Whatever was dilating her pupils probably wasn't helping her focus. "Oh, I suppose you wouldn't know, not being local. I'm the chairwoman for the fall festival– the whole thing was my event. It's why Glenn and I haven't seen much of each other."

"Did you see Terry arrest someone for blood consumption?"

"I didn't see it, no—I was taking a cash deposit to the bank. But I heard all about it when I got back, and how Terry hit Aidan first. About half an hour later, Glenn called me to help keep our local reporters away from the story. I've been working with them to promote the festival, so we have a relationship." Her eyes were watering again, and she'd slurred a couple of her words. This wasn't really the kind of case where they suspected the spouse first, but Ruiz would have had to admit that this woman seemed truly distraught over her husband's death. "That was the last time I spoke to Glenn," she added, sniffing.

"But he didn't come home last night," Ruiz said. "Was that normal for him?"

"No, of course not." She looked a little insulted. "I got a text from his phone, saying he was going to be stuck there very late dealing with the shade arrest business, and I shouldn't wait up. So I didn't. When Kevin came by this morning, he mentioned that all the other spouses got the same text. With the festival and the fallout from that arrest, none of us suspected a problem." She was glaring at Ruiz a bit now, as though he'd accused her of spousal neglect.

Eddy hurried to ask, "So you knew Aidan? Did you think he was—or is—a shade?"

She snorted. "I know the family, yes, and of course he isn't a shade. Aidan is . . ." She paused, appearing to catch herself. "He's unique, in our community," she said at last. "He didn't go to college, for one thing, but socially, he has always been awkward. Harmless," she added quickly, "but awkward. I suspect he falls somewhere on the autism spectrum, but Amy and Dan didn't want to put him through testing." Her mouth turned down in disapproval at this. Ruiz could imagine Mary Holbrook wanting to know everything about a child's disability, and crusading for all of the best treatments. Letting a young man develop in a more organic sense would practically offend her.

"Anyway," she went on, "my husband didn't think he could be a shade either, which is why he did his best to keep the arrest quiet. But Terry had Aidan on a technicality, and even Glenn couldn't deny that." Ruiz saw that her hands were clenched into fists. "This is all Terry Anson's fault. He made those things angry with the false arrest, and Glenn had to pay the price. It's not right."

Chapter 10

Hadley and Faraday hovered in the hallway near the door until one of the nurses shooed them down the hall toward the waiting room. Neither one had to say it out loud, but they wouldn't leave until Amanda Dylan stabilized again.

Faraday, who knew the hospital, led the way to a nearby waiting room, which was currently deserted. Hadley sat down on a vinyl and wood chair, surrounded by ancient magazines and televisions playing CNN. Even in the rich suburbs, some things were the same.

"Breast pads," she said thoughtfully.

"Yeah."

"So we're saying . . . they let her live because she was breastfeeding?"

Faraday's eyes brightened. "Maybe it's like in *Predator II*, when they let the one cop go because she was pregnant."

"I haven't seen that movie. *Who* let a cop go?"

He looked at her like she was slow-witted. "The Predator."

Her phone buzzed, and Hadley saw Ruiz's name on the screen. "Give me a minute," she said to Faraday, and went to the other end of the waiting room to answer the call. She listened to Ruiz's update and nodded. "Got it." She glanced at Faraday, who was staring at one of the TV screens, jiggling his knee. "Let me see what I can do."

She held the phone to her ear for an extra moment after Ruiz had hung up, considering the best way to handle Faraday. Then she pocketed the phone and stalked back over so she was blocking his view of the television, glowering as though he'd personally kicked her dog. "Tell me about Glenn Holbrook and your boss," she demanded.

Faraday blinked, but his expression remained nonchalant. "Christ, that's a waste of time. We should get back to—"

"Humor me," she said, folding her arms over her chest.

He looked at her for a second, then grumbled, "Fine." Faraday tilted his head around in a circle, stretching out his neck—and making sure no one was listening. Then he leaned forward. "Look," he said in a low voice. "I know that back at the station Dennis Lassner came off like a blowhard with delusions of grandeur, and sometimes he can be. But underneath that, he's actually a pretty good cop. And Holbrook gave him this . . . feeling."

"A *feeling*." she said skeptically. "That's it?"

"I know how it sounds. And generally we try not to interfere with the village police unless they ask us. But two different times, Dennis saw Holbrook take a white envelope from a private citizen. The second time, Holbrook didn't know he was watching, and Dennis saw him open it up and look at a wad of cash."

"Did Lassner confront him?"

Faraday nodded. "The chief said it was a donation to a charity that helps the families of murdered police officers—and we *were* collecting donations that month, in both departments. But who donates a wad of cash in an envelope?"

Hadley chewed on her lip for a moment. "That's not much. It's basically nothing."

Faraday spread his hands. "I know. Like I said, I think it's a waste of time. But Dennis has been quietly looking into Holbrook's activities for a couple of years now."

"That's why he wanted the crime scene," Hadley stated. "He wants a look at Holbrook's office."

Faraday nodded. "Specifically his files."

"Our people will take it apart," Hadley pointed out. "We'll get you guys the reports. I play fair."

He held up his hands. "I never suggested you didn't. But we both know that copying us on the reports won't be high on your priority list, and Lassner has been waiting a long time for answers."

Hadley looked at him for a long minute, but Faraday's handsome face was open and serious. "And it didn't occur to you that this could be related to the chief's sudden *violent* murder?"

Faraday shook his head. "Be reasonable, Jill—"

"Agent Hadley," she corrected.

The state cop continued as if he hadn't heard. "I have five different counties to cover. Do you know how many suspicious deaths I have to deal with every year? Even if the chief *was* dirty, it's still Switch Creek. He was probably betting on golf games or fixing parking tickets."

Hadley just gave him a look. Looking defensive, Faraday said, "Come on, you're a fed. You of all people know that crime in Switch Creek is a joke."

"It was," she said acidly, "until last night."

Faraday seemed to droop a bit at that. He reached up and scrubbed a hand through his short hair. "Yeah, you're right," he admitted. "I fucked up."

At that moment one of the nurses poked her head into the waiting room. "She's stabilized," she told them. "Dr. Weber says you are not to speak to her again until she regains some strength."

Faraday, the charmer, stood up to thank her profusely. Then he turned back to Hadley, his face growing serious.

"What do you want to do?"

She regarded him for a long moment, then gave him a thin smile. "Let's give your boss what he wants."

Faraday called his boss, and Hadley made a similar call to McKenna to make the arrangements. Faraday would drive them both back to the crime scene, where he, Alex, and Dennis Lassner would go through the chief's files. Hadley wasn't was going to join them, though, because, God help her, talking about Holbrook had given her another idea. One that she was very much *not* looking forward to.

"Are you sure you're up for this?" McKenna had asked on the phone.

Hadley hated it when he talked to her like she was fragile, so she lied. "I've got it, boss."

"All right, but I'm sending Lindy with you."

"No," Hadley blurted, before she could check herself. "I mean, no offense, but I'd rather do this part by myself."

"Too bad, Agent Hadley," McKenna replied. His voice had gained a little of its authority as a warning, which was at least preferable to his are-you-okay tone. "Lindy might be able to get answers that you can't, and there's not much she can do here to help."

There was a certain tension in his voice, something he wasn't saying about Lindy and the crime scene. Hadley was a good enough cop to read between the lines. Lindy wouldn't be comfortable spending all day around what was essentially her food supply. Gross.

But Hadley knew McKenna wasn't going to change his mind about this. He was oddly protective of the one member of their team who was basically indestructible.

"Yes, sir," she said through her teeth.

Yeah. This was really gonna suck.

Chapter 11

Lindy watched at the door until Hadley and the young state cop pulled up, then she hurried out in her hat and sunglasses, meeting them at the BPI sedan. Faraday gave them a brief wave and headed inside the building to help his boss look through files. Hadley barely looked at him as she broke away and trudged toward the sedan like she was on her way to a hanging. Her own hanging.

Lindy tossed Hadley the keys and opened the passenger door. "That bad?" she asked. Hadley just shrugged.

It was a very quiet car ride.

It was also short. Ten minutes later, they were pulling up in front of the Deerfield Police Department. Hadley still had that look, like she'd been sentenced to hard time. She unbuckled her seatbelt and paused for a second. Lindy waited, expecting her to say something about what was bothering her, but then Hadley just gave a minuscule head shake and opened the door.

Curiouser and curiouser, Lindy thought. Hadley had always been a bit of a mystery to Lindy, a veneer stretched over a hard shell that hid . . . something. Between being preoccupied with Hector and wanting the team to be comfortable around her, Lindy had never pushed. For a moment she wondered if Hadley had been a teenage criminal. Lindy didn't think the Bureau would have hired her with a criminal record, but she had no idea if juvenile crimes applied to that. She climbed out of the car and hurried across the parking lot after Hadley, keeping her head down so the brim of her baseball cap would hide the sun.

"Are you okay?" she muttered to Hadley. The young agent gave her a tight nod, and Lindy gave up.

The Deerfield police station looked much like the Switch Creek station, although it was a little larger and maybe a few years older. Inside, Lindy stuffed her hat and sunglasses into her bag, and they approached a female receptionist in her late forties who could have been Berta Hauptmann's sister. She smiled pleasantly as she looked up at them. "Good morning. Can I help—" Her eyes caught sight of Hadley and widened. "Oh, my God!"

She turned her head and bellowed, "Bill! Get out here! Jilly Bean is here!"

Jilly Bean? Lindy let out a laugh, trying her best to disguise it as a cough. Meanwhile, the older woman was rushing around her desk to throw her arms around Hadley. "Oh, my God, honey, it's so good to see you. How are your folks?"

"They're fine," Hadley said in a subdued voice. "They spend most of the year in Arizona now. I'll see them at Christmas."

Lindy had to work to keep the surprise off her face. Those three sentences contained more personal information than she'd gotten from Hadley in the last two months. She felt her spirits lift a little. This might actually be fun.

A bearlike man of about fifty came rushing through a far door, his arms outstretched as he beamed at Hadley. "Jilly Bean, it's so good to see you!" he said, pulling her in for an embrace. He pulled back and looked her over, shaking his head a little. "Look at you," he marveled. "All grown up and hunting vampires. Damn, girl. It seems like yesterday you were ten and running around this office trying to talk everyone into playing hopscotch."

"Nice to see you, Chief," Hadley said, looking resigned. She turned sideways, stepping closer to Lindy. "This is Rosalind Frederick; she's a consultant with the BPI. Lindy, this is Bill Pike, the chief of police in Deerfield."

Pike reached out a paw for Lindy to shake. "Good to meet you, Ms. Frederick," he said warmly. "Any friend of Jill's, and all that."

"Please call me Lindy," she said with a smile. "But I'm afraid we're here on business. Is there somewhere we could talk?"

He raised an eyebrow. "Sure, let's go on back to my office."

Pike led them through a couple of rooms that were eerily similar to the Switch Creek station, talking over his shoulder the whole time. "We heard that your team was heading over to Switch Creek, of course. Just terrible, what happened. A lot of good cops at that station."

The last room they passed through was the bullpen, and ahead of her, Lindy saw Hadley look suddenly to her right and sort of scrunch her shoulders, as if she were avoiding someone. Lindy glanced to the left and saw nothing but a wall with a large portrait of a young man in a service uniform. A man with red hair. And Hadley's cheekbones.

Lindy paused to read the small brass plate fixed to the frame. *Officer Thomas Grover,* it read, with years for birth and death written below. Lindy did some quick math. Grover had to be at least a decade older than Hadley, and he had died when Hadley was about sixteen. A cousin, maybe?

Suddenly this wasn't so fun. She hurried to catch up with the others.

Chief Pike ushered them into a large, sunny office with

golf trophies on the shelves and a putter in one corner. "Please, have a seat." He closed the door and motioned to two oak visitor's chairs with soft linen cushions. He went around and lowered himself heavily into a leather rolling chair. "Anyway, I wondered if you'd get a chance to stop by while you're in town, Jilly Bean, but I wasn't expecting an official visit." He folded his hands in front of him on the desk. "What can I do for you-all?"

"I wanted to ask you about Chief Holbrook," Hadley said promptly.

Pike's heavy brow furrowed. "Glenn? What about him?" Before Hadley could respond, he added, "Excuse me, but I was under the impression that the murders were a revenge thing. Vampires pissed off about one of their own getting caught."

Lindy was too practiced to flinch at that, but internally, she was annoyed. This was the problem with shades having a reputation for violence—it made people like Pike assume that that was the only reason they'd do anything. Statistically, shades probably killed fewer people than cops did.

"You know how it goes, Bill," Hadley said, and Lindy had to look over at her in shock. Hadley was leaning back in the chair with a conspiratorial smile. "We have to cross all the t's and dot all the i's." Her tone suggested her boss had sent her on a ridiculous errand, and Pike would be doing a favor to help her humor him. Lindy was impressed.

"I suppose," Pike relented. "But it does seem like you're barking up the wrong tree, kiddo."

Hadley's smile flickered and then returned even stronger. "I know. But we did hear that there's a state cop who's got some suspicions about Holbrook."

Pike chewed on his lip. "Dennis Lassner, you mean. Yeah, he's been here asking the same questions about Glenn."

"What was Lassner's reason?"

"He'd seen money exchange hands a few times, and heard a few rumors that were thirty years old. It was nothing."

Hadley pushed her hair behind her ears. "Holbrook is dead, Bill. Nothing you say can hurt him anymore," she said softly. "And there is a tiny chance that this can help us find his killer. What were the rumors?"

Pike shook his head. "Oh, hell, kiddo, it's all ancient history. I won't smear Glenn Holbrook's name and send you on some wild-goose chase." He gave her a patronizing smile. "Trust me, hon. It's the wrong lead to chase." The big man began to rise. "Now, I don't want to keep you, with such an important investigation going on."

Hadley made no move to stand, but she looked at Lindy and inclined her head slightly toward Pike.

Lindy pulled on her lower lip for a second, nodded, and then stood up, reaching across the desk with her hand outstretched. "Thank you so much for your time, Chief."

Humans knew a lot about shade saliva, but they still wouldn't stop the practice of shaking hands, at least not the older ones. Pike reached out to shake, his eyes meeting hers, and she could practically feel the saliva being absorbed into his skin.

"Yeah, well, it's always good to see you, Jilly Bean," he said to Hadley, who still hadn't stood up. "Now . . ."

His pupils dilated. "What was I saying?" Pike muttered.

"You were just about to sit down and tell us about Glenn Holbrook," Lindy replied, forcing power into her voice. It was difficult to mesmerize someone during the day, but she was stronger than most. She would need to feed that evening, though.

"Right," Pike said in a dazed voice. Hadley watched with a sort of detached fascination. "Holbrook. He was the baby broker."

Lindy and Hadley exchanged a glance. "Why did they call him that?" Hadley asked, but Pike's eyes were trained on Lindy. She didn't understand quite why it worked this way, but shade saliva would only make Pike suggestible to her or, in her absence, another shade. She repeated Hadley's question.

"Thirty, forty years ago, starting when Holbrook was in uniform," Pike explained, "Glenn was the guy you called if your daughter got in trouble."

"Pregnant, you mean," Lindy stated. The chief nodded. "Just in Switch Creek?"

"No. Deerfield, too. All the wealthy suburbs from Lake Bluff south to Evanston. Back then, before sex ed was taught in school, old Glenn might get ten or fifteen girls a year with an unwanted pregnancy. Girls from good families, with bright futures."

"What did Glenn do for them?" Lindy said.

"He got the parents in touch with a doctor who wasn't exactly careful with his medical records. If they were real religious and insisted that the girl have the baby, Glenn had a place where they could hide out for the last few months. Then he would arrange a nice quiet adoption and a good cover story for the missing time."

"He sold the babies?" Hadley asked.

Lindy decided to rephrase it for Pike. "He took money for this?"

Pike nodded. "Yes, ma'am. Money from the parents of the pregnant girl, from the adoptive parents, too. I'm not even sure if what he did was technically illegal, but no district attorney would have filed charges anyway. Hell, it was a service for the community."

Hadley didn't bother to keep the look of disgust off her face.

"Was this still going on?" Lindy asked Pike.

His brow furrowed again. "I don't rightly know. Abortion doesn't have the stigma it carried thirty years ago, and kids are more careful now. I certainly haven't referred anyone to Glenn in years, but it wasn't just the police chiefs who knew. Religious leaders, too, and a few of the guidance counselors."

"Jesus," Hadley said under her breath.

Pike's eyes flicked to her for a moment, then refocused on Lindy. "You have to understand," he said, looking a little bit desperate. "A lot of these girls would grow up to marry powerful men, men who wouldn't have liked that they had abortions or gave up babies. What Glenn did, it saved them from public disgrace. He gave them back their futures."

It took a lot to shock Lindy, but this man's casual disregard for the feelings of those teenagers was slimy as hell. She looked at Hadley, who appeared to be thinking the same thing. "Anything else you want me to ask?" she muttered.

Hadley stared at Pike silently for a long moment, obviously weighing something. Then she said, "Ask him if he knows anything about Tommy Grover's death that he's kept from me."

Lindy was surprised, but she did as the agent asked. Pike seemed to think it over for a long moment, but then he shook his head. "I wish I did know more," he said mournfully. "Tommy was a great cop. I miss him to this day."

After that, Lindy went through her usual speech about how he wouldn't remember the conversation, and she and Hadley got out of there. This time, as they passed the portrait, Hadley stopped and paused, her fingers rising to touch the brass plaque.

Chapter 12

In the car, Lindy put on her hat and sunglasses again. The sun was behind the clouds, but it could still hurt her. She waited a few minutes to speak, wanting to give Hadley a chance to sort through her thoughts. Finally, she broke the silence with, "Do you think the baby broker thing is connected to our case?"

"What? Oh. No. Maybe if just the chief had been killed, or even if this had happened on a different night. But I think the first theory is the best." She cut her eyes over to Lindy. "I suppose you'd know more about shade motivations than I would, though. Can you see one of them killing all those people because the local cops arrested that kid?"

"Honestly, I'm not sure," Lindy confessed. "I keep thinking about it, and it seems like too much—an overreaction. I don't think it was Hector, and I don't know any other shades who are brazen enough to kill that many humans at once, and so openly."

"Is there a but?" Hadley prompted. "It seemed like there was a but coming."

Lindy smiled faintly. That was the closest she'd ever heard Hadley come to making a joke. "*But,* I've been out of touch for a long time. And Hector, he was kind of the unofficial leader of the shades . . . or at least he said he was, and no one challenged that. It was *his* plan to stay silent after Ambrose was discovered, and then he turned around and betrayed his own orders by killing all those kids."

Hadley digested this for a few minutes. They were already nearing the Switch Creek exit. "So because of what Hector did, some of the other shades think it's open season on humans?"

"It's possible," Lindy admitted.

They were nearly to the station when both of their cell phones buzzed. Lindy picked hers up and read the text. "Alex wants us to meet him at a sushi restaurant in . . . someplace called Riverwoods?" Lindy checked her watch. It was after one. She still wasn't used to spending all day with humans; she forgot about their constant need to eat. "I guess they have a private back room where we can compare notes."

Hadley nodded. "It's another village, not far from here. I know the place he means."

She checked her mirrors and did a U-turn in the middle of the street. Then she glanced at Lindy. "Thank you," she said stiffly, "for asking Pike that last question."

Lindy nodded. "Your cousin?"

"My older brother. Mom remarried when I was two, and Tommy was eleven. He didn't want to take our stepdad's last name."

"Was Tommy killed in the line of duty?"

"I don't know," Hadley said, and there was a weariness in her voice that spoke of years and years of agonizing over the question. "He disappeared on a perfectly ordinary patrol, right in the middle of a city street. The car was still there, door wide open, nothing on the dashboard camera. Eighteen months later, some dogs found what was left of his body in a culvert by Deer Spring Park." She looked away. "At least we got to bury him."

"Did they figure out cause of death?"

"No. It had been too long."

"So what makes you think a shade killed him?"

Hadley's head jerked around in surprise. "Come on," Lindy said, smiling a little. "I'm not stupid. I heard the FBI team talking about you during the Hector case. You were a rising star at the Bureau, but you walked away from that career trajectory in order to hitch your wagon to a new, untested department at the most dangerous *possible* moment? I've always thought you had a personal stake in getting into the BPI. I just didn't know what it was."

Hadley was silent for a long time, so long that Lindy began to wonder if someone inside the station would see them through the window and come out to see if they were okay. Finally, Hadley said, "You're right. I do think it was a shade. Partly, it's because the cops on the case exhausted every other option *anyone* could think of. I've been through the files. They did a good job."

"And the other reason?"

"There wasn't much left of Tommy's body when they found it," she answered. Her voice was unwavering, matter-of-fact. "But there was enough tissue for the pathologist to determine that he'd been exsanguinated. Years later, when Ambrose was captured and the news about shades came out, the *first* thing I thought of was Tommy's murder. I know it's a cliché, but it was like a puzzle piece clicking into place."

"We don't usually kill humans," Lindy said quietly.

Hadley glanced over, met her eyes. "Neither do we," she contended. "But shade or not, people lose control sometimes."

Lindy tilted her head, acknowledging the point. "Does Alex know?"

The young agent shrugged. "About Tommy's death? He must. It's all in my FBI file, which he would have looked at when he was considering hiring me. But I don't think he knows that I suspect a shade."

Lindy nodded. "When this case is over, I'll take a look at the files on your brother's murder."

Hadley's eyes lit up, but she caught herself. "Really?" she asked in a level voice.

"Yes."

Hadley broke out a full-on grin. Lindy didn't think she'd ever seen her smile with teeth. "Thanks, Lindy."

Lindy kept the surprise off her face. Hadley had used her actual name. "You're welcome, Jilly Bean," she replied.

"We're not making that a thing." But she was still smiling.

Chapter 13

Alex didn't know about the others, but even as he listened to the updates from his team, he could not stop watching Lindy "eat."

He hadn't expected her to order anything at the sushi restaurant, but when the waiter came over she smiled and asked for . . . well, something . . . in Japanese. When the food came, she casually picked up the chopsticks like everyone else and started pushing the pieces of sushi roll around as they all went through their updates.

Then the sushi rolls started disappearing. Alex couldn't figure out where they were going—a napkin? The floor? Eventually she caught him staring and gave him an enigmatic smile.

"They haven't heard from Aidan, and they basically know nothing about last night, other than what's been reported on the news and through the grapevine," Chase was saying. He and Ruiz had just been to see Aidan

Kerns's parents. Chase still looked tired and a little fluish to Alex, but his eyes were brighter and he was waving his chopsticks as he spoke. "According to them, he probably did have autism spectrum disorder, like Mary Holbrook thought, but they never did an official diagnosis. They didn't want to put labels on him, especially because he was so high-functioning." Chase's tone was neutral, but Ruiz made a little face, showing what he thought of that parenting strategy. "He made it through high school and took a nighttime job at a country club, where he mostly maintains the golf carts. I called his boss there, but he doesn't interact with Aidan much. Other than the landscapers, and one security guard, Aidan is the only overnight employee. The supervisor leaves him a to-do list every night, and every morning it's done."

"Okay, so the parents were a dead end," Alex concluded. Ruiz had already filled them in on the interview with Mary Holbrook, and Hadley had walked them through her conversations with the surviving victim and the Deerfield police chief. Now it was Chase's turn.

"Pretty much," Chase agreed. "They seem like decent parents—workaholics, a little distracted, but decent. They're just as baffled as everyone else about how Aidan got involved in this."

Alex picked up another piece of his shrimp tempura roll. "Meanwhile," he said, "Lieutenant Lassner, Faraday, and I tore the station apart, with special emphasis on Holbrook's office. Lassner even spent an hour crawling around looking for loose tiles. Holbrook had a couple of personal files there, but we didn't find anything that stood out as suspicious. Unless Holbrook was hiding things in layers of code buried in different files, I didn't see any evidence that he's still doing the baby broker thing."

"Should we check his house?" Hadley asked.

Alex nodded. "It bugs me that they wrote that message in Holbrook's office, instead of a more public space, so I've got Bartell working on a warrant. Given the circumstances, I don't think it'll take long."

"What about blackmail?" Chase said. "Someone who knows about the baby thing could be blackmailing him, or he could be blackmailing some of the parents. If that person became a shade . . ."

"It's possible," Alex admitted. "I'll get the Bureau's forensic accountants on his financials, see if anything weird was going on. Meanwhile, we stay focused on the shade crime. According to Amanda Dylan, there are three suspects, two males and a female, and likely all of them are shades."

"But how did they find out about Aidan's arrest in the first place?" Lindy asked. "The Facebook video?"

Chase shuffled through his notebook for a moment

and shook his head. "I've had Sarah looking at those videos. She just called me back and said the timeline doesn't work. The arrest happened at 10:15. The police station security cameras went offline at 10:32. But the internet at the town square is a little wonky, so the first video wasn't actually uploaded to Facebook until 10:41, at which point it was passed around and reposted a bunch of times, and a couple more clips popped up too. I know that's tight, but there's no way the shades who attacked could have been tipped off by the videos."

"So the shades must have been *at* the festival," Alex mused. "Ruiz, can you contact Mary Holbrook and see what you can find out about cameras there? Security cams, news people, the Facebook videos, whatever. Then get it to Bartell, and have him and his floaters look through everything and try to separate out some faces we can show to Amanda Dylan the next time she wakes up." He made a note.

"*If* we can get back in to see her," Hadley said, looking a little guilty.

"About the festival," Lindy began. "Last night was just supposed to be the first night, right? This is probably a stupid question, but they're not going ahead with it, are they?"

Alex shook his head. "The state cop, Lassner, told me they canceled the rest of the festival. However, they're going to do a candlelight vigil tonight at the festival grounds, in honor of the fallen."

Several of them spoke at once, but Ruiz's voice was louder than the others. "Isn't that kind of stupid? I mean, there are killer shades running around—no offense," he added to Lindy, then turned back to Alex. "And they want everyone to come out at night and stand around waiting to be picked off?"

Alex held up his hands. "I agree, it seems weird. But they're starting right at sunset and going for an hour and a half, so it will all be over by seven-thirty or so. The whole thing is being organized by the remaining Switch Creek police, and the state cops are providing extra security. We'll need to be there as well, of course, in case the suspects circle back." He hesitated for a second and then added, "It's also possible that the local police are *hoping* the shades come back, so they can get a shot at revenge."

Ruiz rolled his eyes. "That seems dangerous."

"I know," Alex said with a sigh, "but it's like a Take Back the Night thing. They want to feel safe in their own town."

"And none of them really believe they can be hurt," came Hadley's quiet voice. Everyone looked at her. She shrugged. "It's true. The people who live here, they're sheltered their whole lives. They go into the city for a Broadway show or to shop on Michigan Ave. and they think they're cultured, but at the end of the day they live in a bell jar where nothing terrible ever happens." As she spoke, her voice had gotten angrier.

"The murders at the police station were pretty terrible," Lindy said mildly. Alex noticed that her plate was empty except for the remains of one mashed roll. He resisted the urge to poke his head under the table and look for the rest.

"True, but to them, that's a one-time freak tragedy, like a car accident or a lightning strike. It doesn't mean they're vulnerable." Hadley slumped in her chair, poking at her food with one chopstick. "Nothing will convince them that they're vulnerable."

Alex and Lindy exchanged a glance, and Alex realized that Lindy knew about Hadley's brother. Hadley must have told her.

"It could be someone who's back for the reunions," Ruiz offered. "Say they have this ancient grudge against the police force here. Maybe they went away, became a shade, and now they're here for payback."

"All this is just about revenge?" Alex rubbed absently at the scar on his face. When he talked a lot, like today, the part that crossed his lips began to ache. The doctor said the pain would fade eventually. "Maybe. Let's take a look at disgraced or fired cops, people who were falsely accused, anyone with a really bitter trial." He didn't have to tell them that it would take some time, or that their little BPI division didn't really have the manpower to follow that kind of paper trail. The BPI was low on resources, but asking for more resources would mean riling up the public about the possibility of more shade attacks. Which would lead to more political unrest, more retaliations, and, eventually, more shade crime. It was a catch-22.

The others looked a little dejected, and Alex couldn't really blame them. This was their first major case since the Hector thing, and of course it had hit on his first day back since the hospital. Now he felt like he needed to prove himself as the SAC *and* prove that the Chicago pod could handle whatever came at it.

With that in mind, Alex had been hoping to find the killers quickly, preferably before they got a chance to hurt anyone else. But now it was looking more and more like it might drag on interminably.

His phone buzzed, and Jessica Reyes's name appeared on the screen. Alex answered it.

"Give me some good news, Jess," he said tiredly.

"Hey, Alex. I don't know about good news, but I've finished my preliminary report on the scene."

That was fast, but Jessica understood the urgency of the situation. "Hang on, let me put you on speakerphone with the rest of the team."

Alex looked up to make sure the door to the small back room was closed, and put his phone on the table. "We're here, Jess. What can you tell us?"

"Obviously, this is all tentative until I can verify with the autopsies—"

Alex waved one hand in a rolling motion, even though she couldn't see it. "I know, I know, you don't want to guess, blah blah blah your ass is covered, I promise." There was a pause. Hadley and Ruiz were suppressing smiles. Chase shot him a look. Alex amended, "Sorry. Just give us your best guess, please." Reyes was a pro; Alex knew her best guess was the next best thing to set in stone.

Reyes's reluctant voice said, "Well, Ms. Rosalind was right about the varying causes of death. It looks like six of them were killed by a snapped neck, while the rest were bled out."

"Any idea why?"

"Judging by the evidence, it looks like the suspects moved first against those who were carrying guns."

"Huh." The rest of the team, minus Lindy, looked as surprised as he felt.

"Why is that a big deal?" Lindy asked. "Doesn't it make sense that they would take out the armed cops first?"

Jessica answered for him. "Yes, but it also means that at least one of them must have come into the station and looked around to determine who had weapons on them and who didn't. It's more calculated than just rushing the building. Also, judging by the blood spatter and footprints, I'm *guessing* that all three of them came in, left the receptionist alive, and went back into the bullpen. I can't tell who died in what order, but at some point—probably when it got noisy—someone came back out and killed the receptionist before returning to the bullpen."

"They weren't intending to kill everyone when they walked in," Alex summed up.

Lindy nodded her understanding. "And they left Amanda Dylan alive when they realized she had a newborn at home."

"So what happened in between walking in the door and snapping everyone's necks?" Ruiz wondered aloud.

"And why take Aidan with them?" Lindy said. "If they were mad about the false arrest and looking for revenge, why not let him go? It's not like he could have identified them, if they mesmerized him."

"Unless he really *was* a shade," Hadley pointed out. "A couple of people have said no, but we don't really know what might have happened to him in the last few days."

"None of this is adding up," Chase said. He looked as frustrated as Alex felt.

To Jessica, Alex said, "Anything else that can help us out right away?"

"Two possible things. One, the evidence guys looked at the weapons on site. The chief and two other officers got shots off before they were killed. We've got some blood droplets that may be shade. I'll get the DNA testing going as fast as I can."

"All right." Alex wouldn't hold out a lot of hope for that one. The only way to figure out if someone was a shade, aside from exposing them to sunlight or blood, was a DNA test. Ever since shades had become public, every DNA lab in the country, public and private, had become three or four times as busy, as employers at big corporations and law enforcement agencies began insisting on regular tests. More labs were being built, but it was impossible to keep up with the backlog. "What's the second thing?" Alex asked.

"I did put a rush on Terry Anson's bloodscreen, per Gabriel's request. His BAC was point one-one."

"Blood alcohol limit," Alex said to Lindy.

"What's the legal limit here?" Lindy asked them.

"Point oh-eight," said Chase and Hadley at the same time.

"So he was drunk as balls," Ruiz added helpfully.

"Okay . . . does that tell us anything?" Lindy asked.

"I don't know yet," Alex admitted. "Thanks, Jessica. Let me know when you start the autopsies."

He hung up the phone, and saw that a text had come

in from Bartell while they'd been on speakerphone. The warrant on Holbrook's house was ready. "Where do you want us, boss?" Hadley asked him.

Alex checked his watch. It was almost two. His preference would be to send some of them back to the office to work the computers, but considering the commuter traffic, by the time they got there they'd pretty much need to turn around again in order to make it back for the candlelight vigil. "Well, we've got about four hours to kill before the vigil, so let's make them count. Hadley, coordinate with Bartell and put together some photos from the crowd last night. Then get Faraday, go back to the hospital, and wait for Amanda Dylan to wake up again. I want to know what these fuckers look like before the vigil, in case they're not finished yet."

"And if I can't get in to see her?" Hadley asked.

"Call the husband and see what he says." He looked at Chase. "Sorry, brother, but we both know you're better at research than I am. I'd like you to organize Sarah and some of the floaters to research any outstanding grudges against the department."

Chase nodded. "I'll check with the newspapers, too. Sometimes they know more than they're allowed to print."

"Okay. While you guys are doing that, Lindy, Ruiz, and I get to go serve a warrant."

"Cool," Lindy said with a bright smile.

Chapter 14

Mary Holbrook woke up from her chemical-induced nap and for one blissful moment, forgot that her husband was dead. Then she felt the discomfort of pantyhose and the pins in her hair, and remembered why she was sleeping in the middle of the day. And it hit her again with the sharp, tearing impact of a car crash.

She rolled over on the four-poster bed, staring at the ceiling. She was feeling horribly clearheaded, which meant the Valium had worn off. Mary wanted nothing more than to check out for as long as possible, but the bottle was in the kitchen, miles away. Mary wished she hadn't sent the maid home early. Estrella could have fetched the pills.

Glenn.

She couldn't avoid thinking about him. They had loved each other so much, their lives deeply intertwined thanks to their shared values and interests. They never had their own children, but they'd both found satisfaction in caring for the young girls who came to them, and the infants that followed. It was the perfect arrangement, really: spending time with teens and babies, helping them move to the next phase of their lives, while never being tied down to anyone when it came time to take off on the next adventure.

They had been so compatible, in so many ways, Mary thought. She hadn't fully appreciated it until that very moment. Her already-swollen eyes filled with tears again. It had only been a few hours since she'd gotten the news, but Mary already felt like she'd been crying for a week. And there was so much she needed to get done! She had turned off her cell phone, but she could imagine the messages that must be stacking up. How was she going to deal with this?

Pills. The pills would calm her down enough to check her messages.

Still groggy, Mary sat up and swung her legs off the side of the bed. There was a small tear in one of her stockings, and she took a moment to tug them off, impatiently jerking at them as they got tangled in her ankles. When her feet were finally bare she padded out of the bedroom and down the hall toward the kitchen, to find the pills that would dull the pain.

The doorbell rang when she was halfway there.

Mary sighed. One of the neighbors, probably, or her sister, or reporters. For a moment she considered not answering, but curiosity got the best of her. She stopped at the hallway mirror and examined her reflection, taking a moment to wipe at her smeared makeup, just enough to not *completely* embarrass herself. She looked through the peephole, and saw a man in his thirties, wearing sunglasses and a canvas jacket with the hood up to block the wind. He smiled and waved at her with the hand that wasn't holding a wooden clipboard. The temperature was in the mid-fifties, but he was wearing thin leather driving gloves, which she found sort of charming. She opened the door, leaving the chain on.

"Good afternoon, madam," he said genially. He had a British accent, which was charming too. "I'm Corbin Sloane; I'm here to speak to you about the candlelight vigil tonight. My company is supplying the candles."

"Candlelight vigil?" Mary said faintly. She was still out of it. "I don't . . ."

The man looked down at his clipboard. "My information is that you are in charge of the festival, which has now been canceled in favor of a candlelight vigil in the town square. I just need to know where to deliver the candles." He gestured vaguely toward the driveway, which they couldn't see from this angle. At his feet, Mary noticed several flower arrangements that must have been left while she was sleeping.

Mary rubbed her face. She'd assumed the festival would be canceled for that night, of course, but the mayor must have felt that having a vigil would be a good way for the local businesses to recoup some of their losses. It wasn't a terrible idea. "Of course. Please come in for a moment, and we'll sort this out."

She closed the door and removed the chain, ushering the man inside. As soon as he was all the way inside the darkened foyer, he turned to her, reached into his pocket—and pulled out an antique-looking pistol. "Thank you, my dear," he said cheerfully. "Can't have the door showing signs of a struggle, now, can we? People might talk."

Mary gasped, but he was already turning to back her into a corner. There was nowhere to run. His eyes were turning bloody red, and he stepped toward her with his teeth bared and flashing white.

"You can't be a vampire," Mary said stupidly. "It's daytime."

"But I'm quite old," the man replied, his lips turning up in a terrifying smile. "Are you right-handed?"

"What? Yes, but—"

He lifted her left hand, as though he would kiss the back of it, but then brought her wrist to his mouth. She tried to struggle, but his grip was inevitable. "I *am* sorry about this, love, but I have some questions that just can't wait."

And he bit down into her wrist like it was the surface of an apple.

Mary began to scream.

Chapter 15

While Alex knocked on the mansion's big double door, Lindy scrunched herself under the baseball cap, trying to stay in the shade as much as possible. "Mrs. Holbrook?" Ruiz called. "It's the BPI again."

The mansion looked pretty much the same as that morning, although several flower arrangements had been left on the front stoop, next to one of the arches. He looked at Alex, who was frowning. "Did she say she was going somewhere?"

"She may be making funeral arrangements," Lindy offered. "Or helping with the candlelight vigil."

"Maybe." Alex raised his hand to knock again, but quick as a flash, Lindy grabbed it, holding him absolutely still.

"Wait." She leaned closer to the door, and began to sniff at the wood, right about the height of her own head. She stepped back. "Kick it in," she urged.

"What—"

"I can smell shade. They might still be in there."

Alex and Ruiz exchanged a look, and Alex counted to three.

The left side of the door splintered open, and all three of them raced inside. Alex and Ruiz had already drawn their weapons.

"Mrs. Holbrook?" Lindy yelled, cursing the afternoon sun that was dulling her senses. She was trying to follow the shade's scent, but it was too faint, and she wasn't a bloodhound. At least, not during the day.

They each started down a hallway, but before Lindy could get to the end of hers, she heard a door slam from the back of the house. Lindy ran toward the sound, and could hear more feet running in the same direction. Finally she entered a massive kitchen, all steel surfaces and hanging pots, where a vacant-looking woman sat alone at an enormous marble-top table, clutching her left wrist to her chest. Blood oozed between her fingers in a sluggish line. She didn't so much as look up as they approached.

Ruiz reached her first, and crouched down next to the chair. "Mrs. Holbrook? Mary? It's Agent Ruiz again. Are you all right?"

"Hmm?" The woman gave him a vague smile and went back to staring at the tabletop. The men were looking at each other in confusion, but Lindy recognized the signs.

"Tap on your forehead, Mary," Lindy instructed, and the woman instantly raised an index finger and tapped gently above her eyebrow. "That's enough."

Mary Holbrook stopped, and Ruiz and Alex turned to look at Lindy. "She's been mesmerized," she explained. "She'll be suggestible for a little while yet. She'd listen to whoever did this above anyone else, but since he or she isn't here, any shade will do. This must have *just* happened."

Alex eyed the back door, likely the source of the slam. "Ruiz, go see if you can find any signs of the shade."

Ruiz disappeared through the door, and Lindy yelled after him, "Be careful!" Ruiz had been a shade's target once already, and was lucky to have survived.

Alex turned to Lindy. "I thought you had to be *really* strong to mesmerize people during the day." There was real worry in his eyes, and Lindy knew he was thinking of Hector.

"Depends on how you do it." Lindy stepped closer to the seated woman, and gently took her hand, turning it over. "There," she said, pointing. It was a small, half-moon-shaped cut that was already closing. "In order to mesmerize her, they had to break the skin and get saliva right in the bloodstream, which is also why it's healing so fast. During the day, that suggests someone fairly old, but . . ." She looked for the words. It was hard to describe a scale that she just could instinctively sense. "Medium powerful, I guess you'd say."

"But why mesmerize her?"

"He must have been looking for something, either an answer or an actual object. You can still search the house if you want to, but if it was here, he took it with him."

"Can you ask her what he took?"

Lindy sighed. "If I knew what I was looking for, sure. But she won't remember any of her conversation with the shade. Watch." To the woman, Lindy said, "Mary, what's the last thing you remember?"

The seated woman struggled to focus her eyes on Lindy's face. "I wanted my pills," she said plaintively. "From the kitchen. The doorbell rang."

"He wiped her memory," Lindy explained to Alex. "It's pretty standard when you mesmerize someone. Right now she basically has no guile, no defenses. She's like a little kid."

"Hmm." Alex looked at Mrs. Holbrook for a long moment. "Can you ask her if she held something back from Ruiz's interview this morning?"

Feeling like the translator she used to be, Lindy passed on the question, but she could see it was too vague. Of course Mary hadn't told them every single thing about every single thought she'd had. That was much too broad. Without waiting for a prompt, Lindy asked, "Mary, did you lie to the BPI agents this morning?"

She didn't even hesitate. "Yes."

"What did you lie about?"

"Our finances. Glenn has been adding money again."

"Do you know where he got it from?"

She shook her head. Her face began to crumple.

"He's dead. My husband is dead now."

"Did you know about the pregnant teenagers he helps?" Another nod. "Have there been any recently?"

"No. It's been a couple of years." She was crying now, tears and snot streaming down her face without any embarrassment. Lindy went over to the counter and grabbed a wad of paper towel.

"It's okay, Mary." Lindy patted her on the back and looked over her head at Alex.

"Where did—" Alex began, but then the door opened again, and Ruiz stumbled through. He was bleeding from the side of his head.

"Whoa!" Alex and Lindy rushed over and sat him down in one of the empty kitchen chairs.

"It's nothing," Ruiz muttered. "Just a cut. I thought I heard footsteps, but he was waiting for me."

Lindy hung back and let Alex examine the wound. Her control was excellent, but she had been running around a lot during the day, in and out of the sun, and she needed to feed soon. No reason to torture herself.

"This is already starting to bruise," Alex declared. "What did he hit you with?"

"A two-by-four."

Lindy almost laughed. The poor man had been hit by a two-by-four, and he was embarrassed he hadn't done more. "Did you get a look at him?" Alex asked.

"No. Happened too fast."

Lindy risked going over to pat him on the shoulder. "Trust me, it could have been a lot worse," she advised. "Whoever he was, he was trying not to hurt you."

Ruiz gave her a look. "Yeah, that's *just* what this feels like."

Chapter 16

Despite his protestations, Alex ordered Ruiz to go to the hospital and get checked out. He hadn't been mesmerized—Lindy could tell—but he was a little woozy, and the last thing Alex needed was to lose one of his agents. Lindy had offered to heal the injury for him, but Ruiz had backed away from her so quickly that she'd immediately recanted. Alex couldn't really blame him, though: putting shade saliva in his bloodstream would make him vulnerable, and Ruiz was especially gun-shy after Hector's former second-in-command, Giselle, had fucked with his head.

While Ruiz was being examined in the ER, Alex and Lindy checked in with Hadley, who was camped out in a waiting room with Sergeant Faraday and a portable printer. They'd already printed and cut out photos of a dozen faces, and more were coming. "I got hold of the festival volunteer who runs their Facebook page. She posted that we'd like anyone with photos to email them to a BPI account," she explained. "Now we're just trying to get it down to as few photos as possible, so we don't overwhelm Amanda." She handed another bunch of shots to Faraday to sift through. "But we can only eliminate African-American women, minorities who are a race *other* than black—"

"There are about six of us in town," Faraday put in with a wry smile.

"—and people far outside the age ranges," Hadley continued. "Of course, this is all assuming the doctors will let us in to see Officer Dylan when she wakes up again."

Alex flipped through some of the pages. They were mostly posed shots of people bobbing for apples, taking hay rides, or choosing pumpkins out of huge crates. "How many of these are there?" He asked Hadley.

"A couple hundred have come in through the BPI email address already—most people took ten to twenty shots. But there are a lot of repeat faces in there, so it takes time to go through."

He checked his watch. Quarter after four. There wasn't a lot else they could do before the candlelight vigil began, and driving anywhere would give them almost no time at the new destination before they needed to be back anyway. He took his jacket off and looked at Lindy. "How are you at arts and crafts?"

~

Ruiz got an all-clear from the ER doctor ("Just a mild concussion. I've had worse.") and tracked them down in the waiting room. When he saw what they were doing, he reluctantly picked up some scissors and paste and joined in, grousing about "scrapbooking while there were killer vampires running amok."

Ninety minutes later, they'd cut out about a hundred and twenty faces, pasting them to sheets of legal-size white paper. It wasn't exactly pretty, but Alex figured it would do for now. They'd probably just wasted their time, but at least they'd gotten to feel productive. Hadley took the papers down the hall, where she would beg the nurses to let her see Amanda.

"If it's all the same to you guys, I should get back to the town square," Faraday said, checking his watch. "It's almost six. They'll be setting up for the candlelight vigil by now. What time does the sun set?"

"Six fourteen," Lindy said immediately. "I looked it up," she added with an innocent smile.

"All right, then," Faraday said. "Anyway, I'll see you guys there?" But he was looking only at Hadley, his eyes hopeful. Alex suppressed a smile.

"Yes. We should get moving too," Alex said to the others. "I called Bartell; he's gonna meet us there. No such thing as too many eyes."

Alex was still putting his jacket back on when Hadley hurried back down the hall. "The doc said no?" He guessed.

"He did, but the husband took the photos in," she said breathlessly. "Amanda saw one guy right away. He was on the first page." She handed Alex the legal paper, tapping one cutout face, circled in black marker.

He was a fairly good-looking guy with dark blond hair and darker eyebrows, but not anyone you'd particularly notice. Alex smiled at Hadley, trying to keep it on one side of his mouth so it wouldn't look too gruesome. "Nice work."

"Let me see." Lindy stood up from where she'd been collecting scraps of paper on the floor. "No, that can't be right," she said faintly.

"Why not?" Hadley asked her.

"Because I know him."

Chapter 17

The first thing Aidan was aware of was the pain.

Pain wasn't even a good word for it, really. Pain was what happened when you bumped your knee on a table leg, or got a little whiplash from a fender bender. Pain was localized, compartmentalized. It was something that happened to a *part* of you.

This was different. This was everywhere.

It took him a while—minutes, hours, he couldn't tell—but eventually he realized that not only was his whole body in agony, but the torture was different in different places. The pain in his stomach was nauseous and churning, as though his intestines and organs were writhing around each other like a tangle of snakes. The pain in his head was cold and piercing, and sort of jerky, like plugs being yanked out of electrical outlets and jammed back in too hard. His skin felt like it was turning to stone. And his extremities were on fire. His fingers and toes, his shoulders, his calves, even his buttocks, seemed to burn eternally. His arteries and veins were rivers of flames.

Eventually, of course, he realized that he shouldn't be able to feel his own arteries and veins. That was his first real thought.

Then his mouth was being opened, and something warm and thick poured into him. It was like drinking liquid jewels, the taste was so rich and vital.

Eventually, his eyes opened, the pain began to fade, and a picture formed in front of him. It was just a plain white wall over a dull gray carpet, but it was the crispest, most detailed picture he had ever seen. No high-def or plasma television in the world projected this sharply. Aidan was fascinated, his eyes flicking around to collect new information. He was in a large, rectangular room made of whitewashed bricks. There was no door, just an open doorway, at one end of the rectangle.

Then a figure stepped into his view, perfectly outlined against the white wall. He spent a moment marveling at all the enhanced colors and textures before he could process what he was seeing: a young woman, maybe mid-twenties. She had olive skin and black hair that had been shaved on one side, leaving a curtain of glossy mane draped over the other side of her head and part of her face. She wore beat-up jeans and a green military-style jacket over a plain black T-shirt, but the details seemed to explode out at him—the tiny changes of color in the denim, the fading at the seams of the jacket, the obvious softness of the shirt.

She squatted down in front of him, and began to speak. Eventually, he remembered how to process words. ". . . found that it works best not to have too much stimulation right after. Oh, there you are."

Aidan blinked. The young woman grinned, but it was not comforting or amusing. It was a little scary. "Welcome back. Well, *back* might not be the right word. What's the last thing you remember?"

Aidan remembered that if he did something with his lips and voice box, he could make sounds too. "Beer," he managed to say. Then, with great effort, "Drinking a beer. The festival."

The woman nodded. "There's usually a bit of memory loss with transmutation. It might come back, might not. I'm Reagan."

He struggled to say his name back, but she shook her head. "It's all right; I know who you are. I bit you."

"Why?" It came out reasonably clear and understandable. He was proud of himself.

Reagan sat down against the wall, crossing her legs. With his enhanced sight, Aidan couldn't help but notice the extraordinary grace with which she moved. He found he was also able to sit himself up against the wall, mirroring her. "Well, I guess because you asked me to," she said at last.

"I did?"

"I offered you a choice: Join or die. Kind of a cliché, really, but I thought it would be poetic justice. I heard you tell the cop who arrested you that you were guilty." Her eyes narrowed. "I'm not a tremendous fan of wannabe humans claiming to be shades."

Aidan remembered the punch now, the bleeding nose. Remembered Terry Anson throwing him against the tree. "I was arrested for licking blood off my arm. I *did* lick the blood," he said, struggling to explain. "It was gross, but I didn't want it . . ." Aidan trailed off for a second, because his brain had gotten stuck on the words *it was gross*. Because blood wasn't gross, not anymore. It was nectar. It was *everything*. "To get on my shirt," he finished absently. He looked down at his clothes, which were wrinkled and dirty. His tennis shoes were smudged with dirt and grass stains. Aidan felt like he should care very much about this, but he couldn't really remember why.

The scene at the police station was starting to come back to him—not as it had been, but through the lens of his new, clearer ability to make memories.

Terry Anson had marched him into the police station,

still stinking of alcohol. An older man had come out and yelled at Terry in return, until the older man had all but dragged Terry into a side office. The remaining cops had let Aidan sit down next to a desk, but no one had taken off the handcuffs right away. Aidan was uncomfortable, and his nose was still sluggishly leaking blood.

Then a female police officer with blond hair had come over with some tissues and unlocked his handcuffs, then re-locked them in front of his body so he could hold the tissues to his face. She'd patted him on the shoulder before she turned to go back to her desk. Aidan had liked her.

The other police officers were talking and joking in sort of a nervous way. They kept a wide berth around him, although he didn't understand at the time that they thought he might be a vampire.

Then the door opened, and three people entered quietly. Aidan noticed them, because Aidan noticed most things, but nobody else paid any attention—they were focused on listening to the argument while pretending they weren't listening to the argument. The young woman—Reagan—gave him a look he didn't understand, and she and the other two moved around touching people, murmuring to them. Afterward, each person seemed to turn into a statue. But no one touched Aidan. They ignored him.

Soon the three newcomers had touched everyone but the older man and Terry, who were still arguing loudly in the office. Reagan and the others stood on either side of the door, listening. Aidan thought they were probably going to wait until Terry and the older man came out, and then they would touch them, too. He wondered if he should warn the police. But nobody seemed hurt. They were just . . . standing still. Aidan was confused.

"He's guilty!" Terry was yelling. "The little retard told half the village that he drank blood—"

"I don't care!" the older man shouted back. "You're drunk, and you hit that poor kid in front of a hundred people! You're fired!"

"You can't fire me," Terry replied, and his voice was lower now. Aidan, who had been bullied countless times, recognized this as being more dangerous than shouting. "I know way too much about you." For the first time, Terry looked up at the door to the office, which was cracked open. He strode over to close it—

And the young woman, Reagan, was suddenly there. Her arm moved very quickly, and suddenly Terry Anson's nose seemed to explode into a red mess. "That's for using the word *retard*," she said over the sound of his screaming. "Honestly, I thought this town was supposed to be evolved."

The older man was staring at her in shock. He started

to move forward, but she said, "I wouldn't if I were you, Chief."

"Her eyes are red! They're vampires!" Terry screamed, and he ran for the office door. The black man who had come in with the woman moved into the doorway and extended his arm, clotheslining Terry so the bleeding man's legs flew in front of him and he landed on the ground with a *whump*. The black man froze, and looked at his arm with a strange new fascination, as though it had moved by itself. Aidan could see the blood smeared on the black man's jacket, and wondered if he hated getting his clothes dirty, like Aidan did. But the man hissed like a cat, burying his face in the stained sleeve.

The other man, the white man with the dark eyebrows, left his post next to the door and darted forward. "Coop, wait—" he said in a warning voice, but the black man was leaping, four feet into the air at least, and landing on the flailing body of Terry Anson, who looked more than anything like a bloody, upended turtle.

"Cooper, don't—" the young woman cried, and she took some very fast steps toward her companion, but just then the chief drew a gun out of his holster and fired it three times quick-quick-quick at the woman, who turned and hissed too—

And then it descended into chaos, as sound of the gunshots seemed to activate some sort of deeply ingrained instinct in the people who had been frozen. They shook themselves free and turned on the newcomers.

After that, Aidan could only remember flashes of images. Horrible images.

Then suddenly it was quiet. And the young woman's face was right in front of him, *smelling* him. Blood was splashed and spattered on her face and neck, but Aidan did not yet know how wonderful the blood was, and he was repulsed. She had asked him a question, and the others were urging her to leave because of the noise, and then everything went black.

Back in the here and now, Aidan realized that the pain was almost completely gone. He touched his nose, which felt perfectly fine. So did his wrists where they'd put the handcuffs. In fact, he felt remarkably well. "You killed those people," he said to Reagan.

"Yes."

"Because of me?"

Her facial expression changed again, but he didn't know what it meant. "A little because of you, and a lot because of some other things."

He thought about that for a moment. "What happens now?"

She winced. "It's too late to undo what happened, although for the record, I'm sorry I didn't talk to you more before I transmuted you. You don't seem . . . well, I thought you were a different kind of person."

"It's okay."

She raised an eyebrow. "Is it?"

"I wasn't doing much anyway."

A tiny smile appeared on her lips. "You're not afraid of me, are you? And you don't seem freaked out."

"No. I'm not freaked out."

"Why not?"

Aidan shrugged. "Freaking out won't stop you from doing whatever you're going to do to me."

"What makes you say that?"

"It never has before."

Aidan felt someone approaching, though he didn't fully understand how he knew. A man ducked his head in, and Aidan recognized the white man who had helped Reagan at the police station. He held up a hand to Aidan. "Hey, kid. Welcome to the Island of Misfit Toys. I'm Sloane." He had a British accent. "I see you've met our fearless leader." And he looked at Reagan the way Aidan's older brother sometimes looked at him. Fondness and pride.

"Thank you. Why do you smell weird?" Aidan asked him. "And why can I smell you from here?"

The guy blinked for a second, but his lips quirked up in a smile. "Because I'm a shade. And now, so are you."

"Oh. Right."

The man named Sloane gave him a funny look, but then turned his attention to Reagan. "The widow says they own a hunting cabin in another name, where they used to keep the young women before they gave birth. Any files would be there."

Reagan nodded briskly. "Did you get the address?"

No," he said grimly, and Reagan looked disappointed. "The BPI clowns turned up, and I had to erase her memory and run. But she did say that the chief kept a file with the deed and a spare key. It's at the station."

"Of course it is." Reagan paced a few steps away, then back again.

"I'm sorry, Rags," Sloane added. "If I'd had more time—"

She turned to flash him a smile. "It's all right. I know you did the best you could. But we're going to have to go back to the station."

"I drove past on my way here. The press are still camped out at both doors, and there are news vans roaming all over town, not to mention those bloody BPI agents are in town. We may need to do this another time."

"No, that's exactly why we need to go right now." She checked her watch. "I read online that they're doing a candlelight vigil tonight. Most of the town will be there, and anyone left at the police station won't be expecting us to return so soon, if at all."

"I still don't like it," Sloane argued. "Those BPI guys aren't fucking around. This was supposed to be a quick errand."

She sighed. "I know. But we can't quit now. We're so close."

Aidan smelled another vampire, and then the black man from his memories peered around the corner. "Hey, Reagan," he said, his eyes fixed on his shoes. "Look, about last night . . . I'm really sorry."

"It's all right, Cooper," she said, going up on her tip-toes to give the larger man a hug. "You're new to all this. I shouldn't have expected so much from you, so soon. But I do have something else I'd like you to do tonight, if you're up for it."

"Anything," the man named Cooper said. "What do you need?"

She looked from him to Aidan, and this time Aidan recognized her expression, because it was sad, like she had to do something she didn't want to.

"A diversion."

Chapter 18

In the middle of the hospital waiting room, Lindy stood staring at the picture. "I met him in Budapest in the 1930s. I can't remember his name, but he's British, or at least he was using a damned good British accent." The man had been a thief working for a warlord, and he'd accidentally run afoul of Hector. Lindy had taken pity on him and put him in contact with people who could get him out of the country during daylight hours. "But this doesn't make sense," she added, mostly to herself. "This guy isn't a crusader. He wouldn't give a damn if the cops arrested Aidan. He's a soldier. A gun for hire."

"How sure are you about that?" Alex asked her.

"I'm positive."

"So maybe someone hired him to help break out Aidan Kerns?" Ruiz volunteered, then shook his head, wincing at the resulting pain. "No, that's dumb. Nobody knew that asshole cop was going to arrest Aidan. No time to hire help."

"So what *does* it mean?" Hadley asked.

Alex checked his watch. "It means we need to get back to the police station. Let's continue this conversation in the car."

"I'll meet you guys out front," Ruiz said. "Gotta stop back at the ER for some meds." He glowered at Hadley. "Do *not* leave without me."

$\sim$

To Lindy's relief, Alex let Hadley drive, since she knew the town best. They hit a patch of post-workday traffic, and she kept making little disgusted noises at the drivers who cut her off as they bolted off the highway, happy to be returning home.

"Okay, why the police station?" asked Ruiz.

Alex was riding shotgun, but he turned halfway in his seat so he could address Lindy and Ruiz, too. "So this guy," Alex began. "If he was at the police station working for someone, they couldn't have been there for Aidan. They were there for something else. Maybe something from the evidence room or the files."

"But it seems unlikely that they would happen to break in looking for something on the same night Terry Anson arrested a shade," Hadley pointed out. "We've said all along that that's too big a coincidence."

"True." Alex looked momentarily deflated.

"How good was the security at the station?" Lindy asked.

The BPI agents glanced at one another. "I saw an alarm system at the doors and windows," Alex said. "Heavy doors, and the locks looked solid."

Hadley swerved to avoid a jaywalker chatting on his cell phone, cursed quietly, and added, "These rich villages have a lot of toys, even for the police department. Everything will be state-of-the-art, and probably connect directly to the all-night dispatcher at the state police. They can get a car there fast."

"What are you thinking?" Alex asked Lindy.

"Say you're looking for something at the police station, but you don't know where to find it, exactly," she said. "You might show up at the end of the last shift, when people are leaving."

"Meanwhile," Alex added, catching on, "the town is so busy with a local festival that they don't notice some of the cops getting home late, or the extra activity at the police station. Anyone driving by and seeing the lights would just assume the cops were still working."

"All this time, you guys thought Aidan was the connection," Lindy said. "But what if the common thread between Aidan's arrest and the shade murders was actually the festival? If it were me, I would go to the festival beforehand, find a cop, and mesmerize him to take me back to the station, so I could walk in without attracting attention. If these guys did something similar, and they saw Aidan get arrested, they might want to move up their timeline. *Oh.*"

Lindy felt it then: the thick awakening of every part of her body. She took in a breath she no longer needed, and opened eyes she didn't remember closing.

"Damn, woman," Alex said.

"What?" Lindy said.

"What?" Hadley echoed, looking in the rearview mirror.

"We've just never been this close to you at sunset," Ruiz mumbled. He was actually blushing.

"Do I really look that different?"

"Um, you look kind of . . ." Alex seemed at a loss. "I mean, not that you weren't attractive before, but, um . . . Hadley? Bail me out?"

"Sorry, boss," Hadley said in a deadpan voice. "I'm *very* busy driving."

Smiling, Lindy stretched, as much as she could in the backseat, and took in a breath through her nose, taking in all their familiar scents—but there was something else in the car too. Surprised, she looked across the seat. "Ruiz? Is that what I think it is?"

Still blushing, Ruiz reached into his coat pocket and

pulled out a small bag of O negative. "You charming bastard," Alex marveled. "You stole a blood bag for her?"

"Yeah, well, apparently the cops in this town like arresting shades," Ruiz said defensively. "I didn't want her getting caught and having a whole incident. Oh. Here." He reached into the pocket again, and pulled out a paper-wrapped drinking straw. "I mean, I don't know how you usually do it," he mumbled.

Lindy beamed at him. She was genuinely moved by the gesture—even if cold bagged blood tasted like wood chips. "Thank you, Ruiz," she said, poking the straw into the bag. She slouched in her seat and turned toward the window. "Keep talking so I don't feel weird," she ordered.

"Okay, people, back to the case," Alex said, straight-faced. "Nobody stare at Lindy while she attends to her body's needs."

Ruiz snorted. "This is like when you're on a stakeout and your partner has to pee in a bottle."

"Ew," Hadley muttered.

Lindy wasn't really listening. She could get sustenance out of bagged blood, but that meant forcing herself to down it, when her gag reflex was suggesting it would be better to puke it up and start over with living blood. Lindy plugged her nose and choked it down as fast as she could. Then she clapped her hand over her mouth and held it there, waiting for her stomach to stop trying to upchuck.

Alex saw the look on her face. "So . . . not delicious, then."

She shook her head, not confident about taking her hand away.

"Anyway," Alex went on, "the bottom line is that whatever the suspects wanted from the station, they probably didn't have time to get it. Not if there were gunshots, and they decided to smuggle Aidan out of there."

Lindy nodded and moved her hand long enough to say, "If they lost control and drank everyone, they wouldn't stick around to search the place. They would run."

"Which means they have to go back," Hadley concluded. "Okay. I get it."

Alex's cell phone rang. He answered it with, "Hey, Chase"—and then proceeded to listen for a long time. "Get him out of there," he barked. "I don't know, anywhere. We'll be there in—" He looked at Hadley. "Switch Creek town square?"

"Two minutes."

"In two minutes," Alex said into the phone. "Do the best you can." He hung up, and before he'd even lowered the phone to his lap, said, "Change of plans. We have to get to the town square. Chase and Bartell are already there. Apparently there's a riot."

"What happened?" Hadley said.

Alex looked grim. "If Aidan Kerns wasn't a shade be-fore, he definitely is now. And someone just dumped him in the middle of the candlelight vigil."

Chapter 19

Lindy was too surprised to respond right away, but Hadley and Ruiz both started arguing at once. Alex raised a hand. "Stop! I realize it's probably a trap or a diversion, but what choice do we have? Everyone in Switch Creek is angry, and Aidan's their scapegoat. And how long until he decides to fight back?"

"With his shiny new powers," Hadley muttered.

Lindy looked around at all of them, and pressed her back into the seat, where she could feel the twin push daggers strapped to her back. She'd worn them every day since Hector had escaped. "You guys handle Aidan. I'm going to the station," she told Alex.

He looked surprised. "You don't want to help us?"

"He's a baby shade. They will have fed him in order to wake him up so quickly, which means he's not going to show up ravenous. He'll be scared, and want a way out of there." She didn't say it, but the other three shades were

177

the much bigger threat. "Use four or five of your wide zip ties, and try not to hurt him. I don't think this is his fault."

They were on Main Street now, and Lindy recognized her surroundings. Alex opened his mouth, probably to argue with her, but she abruptly disengaged the lock on the car and rolled out while it was still moving.

With her enhanced hearing, she could hear the cries of surprise coming from the car, and Alex shouting her name, but she paid no attention. The people responsible for all that carnage at the police station were back, and Lindy did *not* want them to get away this time.

She pulled on her power, using a speed earned by many years of life, and by the little red bag she'd drunk in the car. It wasn't quite Superman-fast, but she stuck to the shadows, and it was unlikely that any humans would see her as more than a gust of wind ruffling the shrubbery.

The media vans had left the police station—probably they'd moved to cover the candlelight vigil, or possibly been mesmerized to go away—but the lights were on inside the building. Presumably anyone passing by would assume the BPI was still working, but Lindy knew better.

The door was locked, but she pulled back her foot and kicked in the long, thin panel of glass, reaching in to undo the bolt. The alarm didn't sound, which meant it probably hadn't been set when Jessica's team had left for the day. They wouldn't have had the codes.

She walked silently into the reception area. Now that her senses had returned, the whole place stank of death and bowel contents and fear, not to mention a hundred different hygiene products. There was a strong, recent smell of shade, too, but she couldn't tell if they were still here. Lindy hurried forward—and nearly ran into a young female shade trying to leave the bullpen. At the last instant Lindy flipped herself sideways and swept her foot in a sort of backward hook, tripping the girl. She came up with a push dagger in each hand.

"Stop!" Lindy shouted, pointing one knife at the girl, and one at the man behind her. He was the shade from the picture. "Don't move."

There was a moment of frozen tension. The girl just seemed confused, but the male shade's eyes went wide. "*Bloody hell,*" he muttered. He dropped the manila folder he was holding and bent one knee to the floor, lowering his head. "I apologize, my lady. I didn't know you were involved in this."

Lindy had expected to see him, but she was surprised by his reaction. It had been a long time—a *long* time—since her status had been acknowledged by one of her own. She had been in hiding, and before that, many of them had been wiped out during Eradication. The young female was still on the floor, but her head turned to stare at him in surprise. "Sloane?" She looked from his kneeling form to Lindy, and back at the Brit. "Who is this?"

"Rise, please," Lindy murmured, and Sloane practically leapt up, bouncing on the balls of his feet. The woman stood too.

"My lady, this is Reagan. Reagan, this is Sieglinde." He kept his eyes on Lindy throughout the introduction. "She's . . . um . . ."

Lindy found herself perversely interested in what he was going to say. She lowered her push daggers to her sides. "Go ahead."

"She is queen," Sloane said simply.

"Queen of what?"

"Of us, I suppose. She is eldest among us."

"*Really.*" The young woman did not seem impressed by this. If anything, she seemed . . . angrier. She began to prowl a slow circle around Lindy, which the older shade ignored. "Technically, I'm second eldest," Lindy said, her tone mild. "My brother Hector is older by about eight minutes."

Sloane gave off a sudden whiff of fear. "He's not . . . *with* you, is he?"

"No. Hector only cares about Hector." She turned her gaze to the woman. She was young, for a shade, maybe ten or twenty years past her human life. She probably could stay awake for part of the day by now, but she wouldn't be able to go outside in the sun. "But I'd like to know why the hell you decided to massacre the better part of a police department."

"*Me?*" The young woman was incredulous. Her hands were clenched in fists. "What the hell are *you* doing? Our kind is being hunted! They want to dissect and exterminate us! And where is our leadership? Where is our *queen?*" She threw up her hands. "Where have you been?"

Lindy did not answer her, because she did not have to. She may have had complicated feelings about her relationship with shades, but she owed this young woman nothing. "Who transmuted you?" she asked Reagan.

Reagan glowered. "What an excellent question."

"You were abandoned?"

"I was *attacked,* and left."

"Where?"

Now the girl was looking a little thrown. She had obviously expected to be in charge of this excursion, and Lindy wasn't following her script. If she had even a little awareness, she would be able to feel the power humming off Lindy, and know to be careful.

"In Chicago," she said at last. "Sloane found me rolling homeless people for blood, sleeping in sewers. He saved me."

"You saved yourself, love," Sloane said quietly. A small smile played on his lips. His head was still bent respectfully toward Lindy, but she could tell from his expression that he was at least a little in love with Reagan. "I just helped you find a place to shower."

"Why kill these people?" Lindy said, trying to get them on track. "What purpose did it serve?"

Reagan smirked at her. "Besides damn good eating?"

Lindy didn't even have to move. Sloane hurried over to the younger shade and took her arm. "Enough, Reagan," he hissed. "You do not want to make this woman your enemy."

"This woman made *me* her enemy," Reagan said, tugging her arm free, "when she refused to step up and be a fucking leader." She turned to face Lindy. "I've heard about you, but I do not recognize any authority you think you have over me."

"That sounds prepackaged," Lindy replied, frowning. A terrible suspicion had dawned on her, but she really didn't want it to be true. "Who is putting words in your mouth, puppet?"

The young woman crossed her arms over her chest and glowered, saying nothing.

"Fine," Lindy said. "I'm not asking to be your queen. I'm asking you for some fucking answers so I don't have to kill you or throw you into Camp Vamp, which are currently my two favorite options."

Reagan reared back as if she'd been struck. Camp Vamp was the specially created detention facility in DC, where the BPI was keeping their only vampire prisoner. "So it's true. You are working for them. Like a *pet*."

Sloane, for his part, looked confused. "Who told you about me?" Lindy asked her.

"I don't have to answer you. You betrayed us."

Lindy sighed. "Look around, little girl. We may have been yanked out of the shadows without a game plan, but it's not nearly so simple as 'us versus them.' The world is complicated. And yes, if I thought it would prevent more useless deaths, for shades or humans, I would turn you in."

Sloane said in a quiet voice, "And what if it wouldn't prevent more deaths? Are you here seeking justice, or just making sure it doesn't happen again?" He had taken a couple of subtle steps sideways, positioning himself between her and Reagan.

It was an excellent question. "Honestly? I don't know."

"For what it's worth, we didn't intend to kill anyone," Sloane said. "We just wanted information."

Reagan reluctantly picked up the story. "Then I saw what was happening with Aidan, and I lost my temper. And everything . . . escalated."

"It's true, my lady," Sloane said hastily. Lindy didn't

miss the look of annoyance that Reagan shot at him.

"What information?" Lindy asked both of them.

Sloane looked at Reagan, who lifted her chin but didn't answer. Lindy looked at her for a second. At first glance she seemed like a sullen teenager, but there was a defiance to her that Lindy sort of admired. And she'd obviously inspired loyalty in older, more experienced vampires. Who *was* this girl?

"Okay, fine." Lindy holstered one of the push daggers so she could pull out her phone. "If you're not going to talk to me, I'm going to bring you in."

"He told me you might say that," Reagan said. Sloane shot her a quizzical look. She was reaching for the small of her back. A gun? She didn't really think she could hurt Lindy with bullets, did she? "Cooper?" Reagan called. "Hold her still."

"Who told you—" Lindy began, but there was someone moving behind her. She hadn't noticed him coming, not while the air was so thick with smells. She spun around, knife raised, and brought it down on the outstretched arm of a large African American man, hard enough to bury itself in bone. He howled with pain—and then Lindy felt the prick in her back. Reagan had just wanted to distract her so she could shoot her with a dart.

It was a perfect Hector move.

Frustration and rage boiling up inside her. *Not again!* And then, just before her system short-circuited and knocked her out, a great, desperate cry rose in her mind, and she called out in her head and with her voice at the same time.

ALEX.

Chapter 20

A few blocks away, Alex McKenna was in the process of handcuffing a middle-aged man who was throwing himself at the BPI's own SUV, spitting with rage. They had successfully wrangled a stunned Aidan Kerns into the vehicle. He was covered in scratches and cuts, half-mad with the smell of the blood, but more or less okay. The rest of the town, however, had decided that Aidan was responsible for the murders.

"My best friend was in that station!" the man screamed, thrashing against the handcuffs. The state police had managed to create a little circle of breathing room around the SUV—until this drooling ass-clown broke through. The crowd was so deafening that they hadn't heard him coming. Alex turned to pass him to the nearest state cop, when a word exploded into his mind.

ALEX.

He dropped to his knees, clutching his head. It hadn't

hurt, exactly, but the sensation was so weird that it took him a second to realize what had happened. The voice had been distressed, pleading—and unmistakably Lindy.

He *knew* it.

Lindy had been lying about being able to talk to him . . . which meant she'd only use it now if she were in real trouble.

"Alex?" A few feet away, Chase was yelling his name. "You okay?"

"Take over!"

Before his friend could respond, Alex had pushed the unsteady rioter toward him and waded into the crowd.

"Hadley, go with him!" he heard Chase yell, but he was running now, and he didn't look back for anything.

The door to the police station was hanging open. Alex drew his weapon and entered slowly, checking every corner. It didn't take long to find Lindy, lying on her stomach at the end of the reception room, her arms and legs tucked carefully to her body so she looked asleep. A small dart was buried in her back.

Alex forced himself to look quickly in the rooms beyond her, to make sure this wasn't a trap. There was a mess of knocked-over furniture and discarded files in the room beyond, but no people. He holstered his weapon and dropped to his knees beside Lindy, checking her neck for a pulse.

Nothing.

Was that normal, though? He tried to remember everything he'd read about Ambrose's physiology. He didn't always have a pulse, right? Alex had actually *seen* a pulse beat in Lindy's neck before, though, when he'd been close enough. Why hadn't he ever asked if her heart needed to beat? It seemed like such an obvious question now. "Lindy?"

There was no answer. He pulled out the dart so he could carefully turn her over, cradling her head in his lap.

Hadley came skidding into the room, stopping when she saw Alex. "They darted her," Alex said. His voice came out high and broken. "I don't know what was in it."

Breathing hard, Hadley pulled a surgical glove out of her pocket so she could pick up the dart. Cautiously, she smelled the needle end. Then her brow furrowed and she smelled it again. "Boss . . . I think this is meth."

It was odd, but there wasn't much Alex was prepared to do about it right now. "See if you can figure out what they took," he said hoarsely, jerking his head toward the back room.

Hadley disappeared into the bullpen, and he looked down at Lindy. The vitality that had come into her after sundown was gone now, and she looked both waxy and frozen. "Come on, Lindy. Wake up." He could dimly hear Hadley talking on the phone in the other room, but not what she was saying. He didn't entirely care, though in the back of his mind somewhere, he was aware that he *should*.

After a few minutes—or maybe a lot of minutes, who knew—Hadley returned and hovered over him, looking worried. "I don't see anything obvious, but the file cabinet in the chief's office was dumped out and there are files all over the floor. I called Berta Hauptmann, the office manager, to come see if she can figure out what's missing. She was right over at the vigil; she'll be here in a minute."

Alex finally looked up, focusing on the younger agent. He needed to be in charge again. He was supposed to be doing his job. "Good thinking. What are we doing with Aidan?"

"For now, we're sending him to the state police jail," she replied. "Agent Eddy is in the process of securing a vehicle to drive him to Camp Vamp. He can't fly commercial, obviously, so we need a van that we can make sunproof. Then we'll have to find a driver."

Alex considered the problem for a moment. Everything they'd learned about Aidan suggested that he was a pawn . . . but the crowd of angry people down the street proved that not everyone saw it that way.

What would Lindy want them to do?

"Get the van ready, but see if the state police can hold

him overnight," Alex said at last. "I can't see him trying to escape. In the morning I'll send Bartell and one of the floaters to trade off driving. I want to make sure one of our own people is with Aidan."

Hadley nodded, understanding. As far as they knew, the Chicago BPI pod was the only government agency in the world that employed a shade, which also made them the only one sympathetic to them. Another agency might decide to shoot Aidan on sight. She lifted her phone and made the call.

Right after she hung up, a nervous female voice called to them from the doorway. "Um, hello? Agents?"

"Hi, Berta," Hadley answered. "Come on back."

The office manager was dressed casually, in jeans and a barn coat, with what looked like mustard smeared on the jacket. She brushed at it nervously. "Grandkids," she said, embarrassed.

Alex didn't move from the floor, so Hadley stepped forward. "Thanks for coming. Let's go in the back and look around."

Alex said a quick hello, and they went by him, Berta wringing her hands. "I'm not really sure I can be of help," she was saying to Hadley. "Oh, my, what a mess."

Soon Alex was alone with Lindy again. For the first time he registered her push daggers on the floor next to her. One of them looked clean, but blood had pooled on the edge of the other one and made a tiny puddle on the floor, meaning she'd used it on someone. Good for her. "Where the hell were you keeping those?" he murmured.

He shifted her so she was almost sitting up for a moment, and carefully touched her back on the outside of her blazer. It still took him a second to feel the holster. It must have been made to be practically a part of her skin. He smiled. Even unconscious, she was full of surprises.

At least, he was hoping she was just unconscious.

Checking that Hadley was still in the other room, Alex picked up the clean push dagger and let her upper body rest on his knees, so she was nearly facing him. He touched her cheek. She was so small, for someone who contained so much power. He held his thumb over the point of the dagger, steeled himself, and pushed down. It barely hurt, the blade was so sharp, but blood spurted out immediately.

Wincing, Alex parted her lips and gently touched the wound to them, letting the blood drip in.

"Lindy," he said softly. He could see her swallow once, but within seconds, the shade saliva was healing his wound.

"Lindy, honey, please wake up."

She didn't stir. Alex smoothed the hair away from her forehead and examined his thumb, which was now unmarked. "Crap," he said with a sigh. "I don't know why I thought that would work."

Her eyelids fluttered for a second, then opened wide. Alex's heart leapt. "Lindy?"

"*Motherfucker,*" she croaked, and followed it up with some more cursing in at least two other languages, neither of which Alex recognized. "I cannot believe that happened *again.*" She struggled to sit up, which put their faces very close together.

Alex laughed with relief. "Hi."

She smiled back at him. "Hey, Alex."

"Was this that weapon you were telling me about? The one you wanted to test one more time?"

"I think we can consider the testing phase over," she mumbled, but her eyes were locked on his. She smelled like lavender and vanilla. He expected her to scoot away from him now that she was awake, but she didn't move. "Hector figured out that shade bodies don't know how to handle man-made drugs. Something synthetic, like methamphetamine, can cause a kind of short-circuit."

"So this was . . . what, a system reboot?"

Faint smile. "Something like that. Did you feed me blood?"

"A little," he admitted, holding up his thumb. "But the saliva made it heal up pretty fast."

She took his hand, examined it, and then looked at him with her brow furrowed. "Hey... your pupils aren't dilated. Alex, scratch your head."

"Why?"

She stared at him. "Alex, you're immune to the saliva. You're one of the few."

Alex didn't know quite what to think about that. "Apparently we've both got secrets," he said. His voice came out huskier than he'd intended. "You talked to me, in my head. How?"

"I don't know," she confessed. "I shouldn't have been able to connect with your mind, not without you being a shade."

"But you knew back in the hospital," he reminded her. "You lied to me."

She had the grace to look contrite. "I'm sorry. I wasn't trying to keep things from you, but . . ." She shook her head. "It was just too close to having a fledgling again. That hasn't gone well for me in the past."

"Why not?"

"Because Hector always killed them all," she said simply. Her chin was lifted, but he saw her lower lip wobble.

That explained a lot. "Lindy—" he began.

"Is she up?" Hadley called from the next room. Her footsteps were moving toward them.

They weren't doing anything wrong, but Alex and Lindy instinctively moved away from each other before Hadley approached them. "Hey, Lindy," she said, looking relieved. "Glad you're back."

"What did I miss?" Lindy asked them both. Alex stood up and reached down to help her to her feet. He held on to her hand a few seconds longer than was strictly necessary.

"We caught Aidan before the crowd managed to stone him, but the people who darted you got away," Alex informed her.

"Reagan," Lindy said. "She's the one in charge. Her associates are Sloane and Cooper. Sloane is the one I met before."

"We need to stop them before they hurt anyone else, or get out of Chicagoland. Any idea where they're going?"

Lindy shook her head. "But they might not be our biggest problem. I think Hector's been feeding this Reagan information."

They both stared at her. "Hector your psychotic brother?" Alex asked, at the same time Hadley blurted, "Please tell me you're kidding."

"I wish I were kidding," Lindy said. "But she knew to shoot me with the dart, and she went on about my lack of leadership, which is one of Hector's favorite bits. Besides, Reagan would be such an easy mark for him. A young, natural leader with abandonment issues? She's catnip."

"That might also explain why they left you alive,"

Hadley pointed out. "No offense, but these guys *had you*. But they left you here, alive, without even taking your weapons."

Lindy nodded. "If she is working for Hector, he wouldn't want her to kill me. Hector would be furious if anyone else got to kill me first."

"Brothers can really suck sometimes," Alex said solemnly. Hadley recognized the double meaning and rolled her eyes.

Lindy was looking past him to the mess in the other room. "Did you figure out why they came back here?"

"I think I might know!" Berta Hauptmann called. She had just come out of the chief's office, and was speed-walking toward them. "There's a file missing!"

Behind her, Alex could see into the bullpen, which was covered in a stack of dumped files. "How can you tell?"

"Because this one was special," Berta said triumphantly. "It was a case file, but it was dark green, where the others are manila. And the case name was fake."

"What? Why?"

Berta rolled her eyes. "Because it was the deed and a spare key for the chief's hunting cabin. You know those fake rocks where you can hide a key? He thought he was being so clever by keeping the information in with the files. I never understood the cloak-and-dagger, myself."

Alex looked at Lindy. In his head, she said, *If you were keeping something there that you didn't want anyone else to know about, you might take extra precautions.* She did it so smoothly, like she'd been talking to him that way all his life. It was obvious that she'd once been used to communicating like that.

"The pregnant girls," Alex said softly.

Berta scoffed. "Haven't been any of those in years now."

All three BPI members turned to look at her. She waved a hand. "Oh, yes, I know all about that." She straightened herself up. "I was on the campaign to get sex ed in the schools, and later, to get the kids access to birth control and condoms. I didn't want any more of that sneaking around, making the girls feel shameful and isolated. It's worked, too. I don't think the chief and his wife have hosted a girl for five or six years now, although I might not have heard if they had."

Alex was impressed. He'd obviously underestimated Berta Hauptmann. "Did the chief keep records of the adoptions?" Alex asked her.

She frowned. "If he did, it would be out at the cabin. When he realized how much I disapproved, he cleared all the baby broker stuff out of the office. That was twenty years ago."

"You're thinking this Reagan was one of the babies?" Hadley asked him.

Alex nodded. "That, or one of the mothers."

"No, I think you were right the first time," Lindy put in. "Reagan told me that she never knew the shade who transmuted her. If she was given up as a baby, and then given up again after she became a shade—"

"That would sure as hell make *me* angry," Hadley remarked.

"Exactly. She can't find her elder, so she wanted to find her mom."

Alex turned to the office manager. "What do you know about this hunting cabin, Miss Berta?"

"Well, it's not really a *cabin*, though the chief did use it for hunting and fishing. It's about an hour south of here, near Wolf Lake," she said. "I haven't been there, but one of the detectives went one time to hunt and told everyone about it. It's at the top of a hill, with a zigzag driveway like those train tracks on hills."

"A switchback," Lindy supplied.

Berta nodded. "Yeah, that's what the chief called the place. I suppose it's big enough to need its own name."

Lindy and Alex exchanged a glance, and then Alex turned back to the older woman. "Can you get us the address?"

"I think so. Let me call Kevin. His phone number is in the chief's office."

She returned a moment later with a Post-it note—and

an expression that was far more worried than when she'd left. "Kevin still had the address, but there's something else you should know. While I was in there I thought to check the chief's safe." She swallowed hard. "There are some weapons missing."

Chapter 21

"Two hunting rifles, a shotgun, and three Glocks," Alex told his team. Chase had a scratch on his face, and Bartell looked tired, but other than that, everyone seemed to have survived the candlelight vigil. They were all gathering at the state police headquarters, where Alex's new best friend Lassner had given them the use of the briefing room. "That's what they took. Apparently the chief didn't keep the safe locked during the day, and since he never clocked out last night, it's been unlocked this whole time. No one thought to check it."

"Does this Reagan actually know how to use any of the weapons?" Chase asked.

"She might not," Lindy answered, "but Sloane does."

"We also think that Reagan, at least, is in touch with Hector," Alex told the others. "We need to stop them now, tonight, because there's every chance that after this, they'll meet up with him."

Everyone went quiet. "If we can stop them in time," Lindy added, "we might be able to use Reagan to get us to Hector, and that's what we all want."

They exchanged glances. None of them had forgotten what Hector had done the past summer. Alex figured they remembered every time they looked at his face. "Let's do this," Ruiz said eagerly. Hadley and Bartell nodded with nearly identical steely expressions. Only Chase looked troubled.

When the others went to put on their gear, Alex asked him to hang back.

"Dude, what's going on with you?"

Chase gave him a look of incomprehension. "What do you mean? I'm fine."

"You've seemed off since . . . well, since I was in the hospital, actually. You barely visited, and you haven't been returning my calls, and now you look like shit. Something just feels not right with you." He gestured toward the door. "And we might be going after the big fish. Are you up for this?"

For maybe the first time he could remember, Alex couldn't read Chase's expression. "Of course I am."

"Then what's going on?"

Chase's face hardened. "Look, I'm sorry if I seemed scarce after the Hector case, but you know, you did sideline me that night. Did it ever occur to you that I might be upset about not being able to help you guys?"

Alex was taken aback. "I guess it didn't."

Chase went on, "You dragged me into this BPI gig with you, and then you kept me out of the action. I'm your best friend, I'm supposed to have your back, but every time I look at your face, I wonder if I could have helped. Or if it would have been me with those scars." His fists were clenched.

" . . . Oh." Alex wasn't sure if he should apologize or not. After all, he was the one who'd gotten hurt . . . but he'd never taken Chase's feelings into account either. "Look, let's grab some food tomorrow, just you and me. We should talk. Okay?"

Chase gave him a curt nod, and Alex ended up feeling more confused than before.

~

While the others were packing their gear, Lindy pulled Harvey Bartell aside for a moment.

"Are you sure you're up for this?" she asked quietly.

Bartell raised an amused eyebrow. "Because I'm old?" He finished pushing ammunition into a shotgun, locking it shut.

"Because you have cancer."

He went still, then looked around to make sure the

others were still at the other end of the room. No one was watching the two of them. Bartell put down the shotgun. "I thought we weren't mentioning that."

Lindy had smelled the corruption in his bloodstream the first time she'd met him. Even when he came in late on Friday mornings, stinking of chemotherapy chemicals, she'd kept her mouth shut, figuring Alex probably knew—and if he didn't, it wasn't her secret to tell. Lindy had plenty of practice with keeping secrets.

But Alex wouldn't send Bartell into the field if he knew the other agent was sick. "In front of the others, no," she replied. "But I need to make sure you're going to be able to go out there, against shades."

"I'm not going to get any worse in the next few hours," he assured her. "And we need everybody we can get." He gave her a smile tinged with sadness. "Anyway, I'm the perfect person to go on this mission. I'm expendable."

"No, you're not." She watched his sure fingers placing equipment in his duffel bag, thinking over her conversation with Alex. "I could transmute you," she said finally. "I haven't done it in a long time, but . . . you still have a lot to offer this team."

Bartell froze, and for the first time since she'd met him, the veteran agent looked truly flustered. He opened his mouth to answer, shook his head. Tried again. "I don't think I'm cut out to be a vampire, Lindy."

He'd used her first name. "Just ... think about it, okay?" she suggested. "When this is all over, we can talk."

He nodded, looking pensive. "All right. I'll think about it."

~

They went in a caravan: the SUV in the lead, with Ruiz, Chase, and Bartell inside. Hadley drove Alex and Lindy in the sedan. Lindy had suggested the younger agent drive since she had been to Wolf Lake before, but Alex suspected she just didn't like his driving. They went with lights and sirens for most of the way, which cut the one-hour car ride down considerably.

Alex spent a chunk of that time on the phone with Mary Holbrook. When he asked her why she didn't mention the other house to them, she claimed it had nothing to do with Glenn's death. Alex exchanged a look with Lindy, who could pick up the conversation with her enhanced hearing. "It was where you kept the girls, wasn't it?" Alex said in a calm voice. "In their last few months, when they couldn't hide it anymore, you hid them away at Switchback."

There was a long moment of silence, and then Mary said, "I do hope you're able to find these people before anyone else gets hurt, Special Agent McKenna. I myself haven't been up to Glenn's hunting retreat in many years, so I have no idea what he may have done with the place. Good luck."

And she hung up the phone.

"She's a piece of work," Lindy muttered.

"Would it be paranoid to suggest that she's hoping we all die up there?"

"I think not."

Alex glanced over his shoulder. It was full dark now, but when the headlights of another car flashed by them, he could see that Lindy looked troubled. "You're worried about Hector, aren't you?"

"Yes."

"Do you think he's going to be at Switchback?" Hadley said, looking at Lindy in the rearview mirror.

"I'm about eighty-twenty that he won't. This doesn't feel like one of his big plays, more like a fun little diversion. Putting Reagan on a collision course with me just to see what happens is totally his idea of fun. But if he *is* there," she continued, "your team is going to have to handle the other three shades without me. I'll be quite busy."

Fear lanced through Alex's body. When Hector had been kidnapping teens the previous summer, his right-hand woman, Giselle, had taken out an entire BPI pod by herself. And that was just one shade. "This is worrisome," Alex said out loud.

Hadley raised an eyebrow and looked at him. "I don't suppose you have any meth on you?"

He pretended to pat his pockets. "Left mine in my other pants. But we should talk to Noelle after this, see if she can rig up some dart guns for us."

"That would be nice," Lindy said wryly. She was obviously still annoyed about being darted earlier, but Alex had talked her into wearing a Kevlar vest.

Then they were coming up on the turn for the driveway. It was about half a mile away from the lakeshore, where the land swelled up gently to create natural hills covered in forest.

The radio beeped. "How do you want to do this, Alex?" Chase asked over the line. They had cut the sirens a few minutes earlier. "Park on the road and walk up so they don't hear us, or pull right up to the front door?"

"One of each," Alex said. "Our car will go to the front door. We're gonna knock politely. You guys park here and sneak around back." He eyed the steep hill and added, "Bartell, once they're out of the SUV, move it to block the end of the driveway and wait there. I don't want anyone getting by us."

The moon was nearly full, and Alex could make out most of the property: The trees had been cut back to create a huge clearing, which formed a vertical oval around the house. Berta's information had been correct: the driveway was like a giant backward Z, similar to the way railroads created switchbacks to make it easier for locomotives to get up steep hills. The building at the top was ornate and imposing, perched menacingly on the top of the hill in a way that would allow the house's inhabitants to see anyone coming.

Hadley turned the sedan into the driveway, which veered sharply right, curved left, and jagged right again in order to reach the "hunting cabin." "Jesus," she muttered as the car crawled up the first leg of the driveway and made the first turn. She was going slow, to give Chase, and Ruiz time to climb up the hill close to the tree line. "How much are babies selling for these days?"

"Something's wrong," Lindy said suddenly. "Stop the car." Hadley braked gently, just past the first turn. Lindy pushed at the button for her window. "Did you put the child lock on?" she demanded.

Alex answered, "I did. Because *someone* rolled out of a moving car earlier." But he gestured for Hadley to hit the button so Lindy could get the window down.

"Do you smell that?" Lindy asked.

Alex looked at Hadley, but she shook her head too. "What do you smell?" he asked Lindy.

"Kerosene, I think." Lindy's head was halfway out the window now as she sniffed. "Alex . . . I think it's coming from the house."

"She's going to torch it," Alex said grimly. To Hadley: "Get us up there *now*."

Hadley stepped on the gas, and the sedan lurched forward along the middle part of the Z. They had made the turn and started up the final leg when the house above them exploded.

Chapter 22

SWITCHBACK

FRIDAY NIGHT

It may have looked like a bomb, but after a moment Lindy realized that someone had simply thrown a Molotov cocktail through an open window, igniting a floor that had already been primed with kerosene. The flames leaped up faster than seemed possible, and soon the whole first story was engulfed, and the fire was moving on to the second. She scanned the shrubs near the house until she saw the silhouetted figure creeping away from the window. "There!" she shouted, pointing.

Alex had his gun out and his door open in an instant—and he was immediately forced back into the car, as bullets hit the side panel of the sedan. The shots were coming from a female figure standing at the edge of the driveway, where she had probably hidden behind the shrubs and jumped out when they arrived. Lindy caught a flash of dark hair and green jacket, and recognized Reagan. If she'd waited one second longer, she could have taken off Alex's head.

The next shots hit his window, but couldn't penetrate the special glass. "Can you back us out of here?" Alex yelled to Hadley over the noise.

Hadley put the car in reverse, but before she could even step on the gas, Reagan lowered the gun's muzzle and shot out the tires. It was a cue for the man near the burning house to shoot the tires on the other side. He stopped shooting long enough to rear one arm back and throw something transparent toward the mouth of the driveway. Below them, Lindy saw the object strike the ground, causing the mouth of the driveway to ignite too. No one would be able to drive up and save them. "They're trapping us!" Hadley shouted.

Lindy had to admit, she was kind of impressed. She had underestimated these shades' ability to hurt her. Reagan could just shoot at the BPI sedan forever now, until the glass finally gave out or the gas tank ignited. Lindy could survive many things, but she was as vulnerable to fire as any human.

"Hadley, be ready to raise my window," Lindy said calmly.

"What—"

But Lindy was already leaning on the button, and the glass slid down in the door. A couple of Reagan's bullets came into the vehicle, but Lindy was the only one in the backseat, and she was watching for them. When the window was all the way down, she got her feet up and sprang out of the window, landing on her hands and coming up in a roll.

Reagan stopped shooting and moved backward, dropping off that leg of the driveway to the longer part below. She obviously expected Lindy to chase her, but Lindy recognized a trap when she saw one. Her brother would have expected her to go after Reagan, but catching the other shade wasn't Lindy's priority. She cared far more about saving Alex and Hadley, and she needed to get them out of there before the fire spread.

Lindy raced around the car at her top speed, surprising the large African-American shade who had gone back to shooting at the car. She leaped into the air, landed on his shoulders, and rode him down before he could so much as bring his gun up. When he hit the ground she pinned down his gun hand with one extended leg and held a push dagger to his neck. "How many of you are there?" she demanded. She could feel the heat from the fire warming her face.

"Just—just two," the man sputtered.

"Where's Sloane?"

"He said he wouldn't help Reagan move against you. They fought about it. He left."

Smart man. "What about Hector? Is he here?"

The other shade looked confused. "I don't ... who's Hector? You mean the guy in the newspaper?"

She looked at him closely in the flickering firelight. This man hadn't been a shade long—maybe a year, at the most. If Reagan *was* working with Hector, she probably would have kept him out of it.

Lindy looked over her shoulder at the car, motioning to Alex with her head. He and Hadley climbed out of the useless vehicle, guns in hand. The house was burning hotter than ever—the skin of her face hurt from it—but now Lindy realized with relief that the grass all around it was saturated with water. They'd even dug a short trench, to keep the fire from spreading to the tree line.

Lindy turned back to the shade. "Why did—" she began, but then more gunfire came from behind the car, back by the trees. At least two different weapons. Alex and Hadley took cover behind the car, but the shots kept coming, getting closer. "*Lindy!*" Alex screamed, and there was something in his voice that made her snap to attention. She had never heard him sound so unnerved. "We've got a problem!"

"Coming!" After taking the gun from the shade beneath her, Lindy balled up a fist and hit him as hard as she could. His cheekbone, nose, and one eye socket caved in, making him writhe on the ground. He was young; it would take him a while to heal. Lindy left him there and raced to Alex's side. "It's not Reagan," Alex yelled. "It's our guys."

She craned her neck to peer around the car. Bartell and Ruiz were moving toward the vehicle, each holding a rifle. They were methodical about it, their faces expressionless as they took turns reloading and firing. A shot hummed past Lindy's temple, and she pulled back around the car, crouching next to Alex.

Okay, now Lindy was pissed. Reagan had mesmerized them, like toy soldiers that you wound up and sent into battle. Only she was going to pit federal agents against their friends and trusted colleagues.

Someone was going to get hurt.

Hadley was leaning around the nose of the car, sending shots in the general direction of the pair, just to keep them back a bit. And there was no sign of Chase, which couldn't be good. He could already be dead, or trying to circle around to shoot them from behind.

"I don't want to shoot them," Alex said, his eyes desperate. "Can you get their guns before they hurt anyone?"

Panic flooded into her, along with the memory of Alex lying on the floor in that abandoned clinic, his life pumping out of his body after Hector cut him down. *Oh, God, it's going to happen again. I can't protect them all.*

She hadn't realized she'd pushed the thought into Alex's head until she saw him switch his gun to his other hand. Roughly, he grabbed the lapel of her jacket. "Lindy!" His eyes were fierce and wild. *"You can do this."*

She forced herself to calm down. "Okay. Okay. I'll be right back."

Standing, Lindy raced around the car in a wide arc, circling to come around behind Ruiz first. She snatched the gun out of his hand and threw it as hard as she could toward the forest. Carefully, she hit him just hard enough to put him down.

Unfortunately, she had to hold still to pull the punch, and that gave Agent Bartell the perfect shot at her. Lindy ran toward him to get the gun, but even she wasn't fast enough to stop his first bullet from planting itself in her shoulder, just above the collarbone. And above the Kevlar vest.

They went down in a tangle: her, the rifle, and Bartell. Lindy grimaced against the pain. Her body was already working to expel the bullet and heal the wound, but she wouldn't have the use of her right arm for a few seconds. With her left hand she tossed this rifle, too, but Bartell was already pulling out a handgun. He was fast for his age. She caught it and pushed it above his head, trying to hold his arm there, but the grass was slippery and leverage was not on her side.

"Harvey, stop!" she shouted into his face. All the gunfire would have temporarily affected his hearing, but goddammit, she wasn't a baby vampire. She *would* get through to him. "It's Lindy! Your friend!"

His eyes, wreathed in fine lines, locked on hers, and Lindy felt his recognition like a connection between them. Bartell's arm began to relax. "Lindy?" he said, his voice much louder than necessary. "What just happened?"

She grinned at him. "I'll tell you if you promise not to shoot me again."

He looked confused for a second, then became aware of the gun in his own hand. He let go of it immediately. "Oh, hell, I'm sorry!"

Then Alex was there, pulling her to her feet and checking her over. The front of her shirt and jacket were wet with blood, but she could already feel that the bullet was out. Alex cupped her face in his hands. "Are you okay?"

Lindy had to smile at him. He was just so ridiculous sometimes. "Take care of Bartell. I'm going after Reagan."

She took off in the direction Bartell and Ruiz had come from. Behind her, she heard Alex shout, "Find Chase!" His voice was full of fear.

Chapter 23

THE WOODS NEAR SWITCHBACK
FRIDAY NIGHT

As she ran toward the trees, Lindy's enhanced senses picked up the distant sound of fire trucks. Someone must have spotted the burning house. Good. "Chase!" she shouted. Reagan hadn't seemed inclined to murder people without a good reason, but then, Chase would have tried to attack her. That might seem a pretty damned good reason at the time. Lindy sniffed the air and followed the smell of shade into the woods.

Reagan had brushed up against trees and bushes , not bothering to conceal where she was going. Lindy ran as fast as she could, but the younger woman had gotten a head start. She could run until sunrise, and who knew what Reagan might do if she panicked and needed a place to hide out during—

Lindy almost tripped over her.

She had reached a small clearing, and to her left, a small figure huddled under a tree, staring at an open file that rested on her knees. She didn't even look up as Lindy approached.

"Reagan?"

"Yeah." The young woman didn't look up. "Is Cooper okay?"

"I hit him really hard, but yes, he'll be fine."

Reagan nodded. "She's dead," she said flatly. "Breast cancer, ten years ago. She was only thirty-seven."

It felt surreal, but Lindy went over and cautiously sat down across from the young shade, folding her legs in a lotus position. "Your mother?"

Reagan nodded. Lindy could see tears shining on her cheeks, catching the moonlight. "I thought . . . I don't know what I thought. I had this big decision to make, and I guess I figured knowing where I came from might help me. I could meet her, and we could have a really good talk and I could make her forget about it. No one would get hurt . . ." She trailed off. It was painfully obvious that plenty of people had gotten hurt.

And then Lindy understood. "Hector offered you a place with him."

"He promised me things," Reagan said in a small voice. "That he would take care of me. I wouldn't be on my own anymore. I wouldn't have to keep everyone else together. I could have money and a place to live, and he would teach me about what we are. Make me more than I've been.

"But he encouraged me to do this first. He thought it would be good for me to find my mom."

All the anger that Lindy had built up toward this young woman was already fading away. "No, he didn't," she said wearily. "He wanted to test you, by sending you against me. This was your audition."

For the first time, Reagan looked up and met Lindy's eyes. "Do you think I passed?" she whispered.

∿

Reagan didn't resist as Lindy gently moved her hands behind her back and started pulling zip ties out of her pocket. If anything, she seemed a little relieved. Lindy layered the ties around the girl's wrists, one over another, until she was satisfied that *she* wouldn't have been able to pull them apart. She checked Reagan for blades, to make sure she couldn't cut herself free, and then stepped around to face her. "Where's my other colleague?" she asked the girl. "Chase Eddy."

Reagan stared at her blankly for a moment, then her face relaxed. "Oh, him. He's tied up to a tree, about a hundred yards that way." She nodded north. "Hector wanted him to stay out of this."

"Why?"

Reagan shrugged. "He didn't say."

Lindy pulled out her phone and called Alex, relaying the information. She considered it for a moment, then decided to zip-tie Reagan's legs as well. It would mean carrying her through the forest to return to the others, but Lindy was strong, and she didn't really trust the girl not to run.

"What's going to happen to me now?" Reagan asked in a small voice.

"You'll go to prison. That's what happens when you kill people."

"What about Cooper and Aidan?"

"Cooper will go to Camp Vamp too. I suppose Aidan will have to go as well, even though he was kind of the victim here."

"I know. I've spent years finding shades who'd been abandoned or lost, helping them get on their feet again. A couple of times I transmuted someone who was about to die, like Cooper." She shook her head. "But I made a mistake with Aidan."

"You're young," Lindy said simply. "And if there's one thing Hector knows how to do, it's shape people into what he wants."

She stood Reagan up, preparing to hoist her over her shoulder, but then a phone in Reagan's jacket began to vibrate. Her eyes widened. "That's him."

Hector. Lindy patted her jacket and pulled out the

phone. The number was blocked.

She answered it. "Hello, Hector."

Only the briefest pause. "Lindy! I see you met my new acquisition."

She looked at the girl, who had let herself collapse back down to the forest floor. All the fight had gone out of her.

"What the hell, Hector?" Lindy said angrily. "There are plenty of qualified shades you could have reached out to, but you picked a girl who was practically in my backyard?"

He laughed, and she knew instantly that she'd made a mistake. She'd given him the exact prompt he wanted. "You took what was mine," he said, his voice calm but reproachful, as if she'd stolen his dessert. "So it seemed only fair that you should suffer in replacing her."

The penny dropped. "Giselle? All *this* is because I killed your pet psycho?"

"Show some respect," he snapped at her. There was a beat, and in a calmer voice, he added, "Giselle may have had her flaws, but she was infinitely useful. And Reagan will be too, now that you've helped me break her down. I can build her into so much more than she's been."

"I won't let you," Lindy said tightly.

"Oh, little sister," he said, his tone patronizing. "When have you *ever* been able to stop me?" And he hung up.

The phone splintered in Lindy's hand.

Chapter 24

Alex spent the next three hours talking to firefighters and paramedics and the state police. Faraday and Lassner had arrived about fifteen minutes after the BPI team, but by then there was nothing to do but guard the zip-tied Cooper and watch the house burn to the ground. Alex checked on his team members, then went down to the SUV and picked up Lindy where she emerged from the forest onto the road, with Reagan slung over her shoulder. Lindy seemed even more quiet and troubled than before. Alex let her wait in the car with her prisoner while he finished up at Switchback.

The fire on the driveway had already burned itself out, and the fire teams thought they could keep the blaze contained to the house. Alex wasn't sorry to see it go.

Chase was fine, although he was mad as hell about being left out of the action again. As penance, he offered to take over on-site coordination, so Alex could get the captured shades out of there. Reagan, Cooper, and Aidan would spend the rest of the night at the state police headquarters under heavy guard. Hadley had volunteered to be part of the guard detail, even after Alex tried to send her home. Privately, he wondered if her decision had something to do with Faraday, who was also staying to help, but it was none of his business. In the morning, Bartell and a floater would drive the three of them to DC. Camp Vamp was about to have three more occupants.

Ruiz elected to stay and help Chase finish things up. The man looked exhausted, but Alex thought he was probably not ready to see Lindy. He seemed embarrassed about being mesmerized again, and about attacking her.

With Lindy's help—and, okay, her protection—Alex delivered Cooper and Reagan to the state police. Lindy made a few attempts to get more information about Hector out of them, but both shades were subdued and uncommunicative. After talking to Hector on the phone, Lindy didn't bother to push it—Hector wouldn't have told Reagan where he was.

As they were pulling into the state police headquarters, however, Reagan finally spoke. A little of the fire was back in her voice as she said, "Soooo . . . When we get in there, what's to stop us from telling everyone that their BPI 'consultant' is really the queen of vampires?"

Alex and Lindy exchanged a look. With everything that had been going on, Alex hadn't considered the possibility of someone exposing Lindy's secret identity.

Lindy didn't even turn around in her seat. "First," she

said in a voice that was very soft and very dangerous, "I would ask yourself if that's really what Hector would want. If he wanted my identity exposed, wouldn't he have done it himself by now?"

Some of the smugness left Reagan's expression. "Second," Lindy continued, "there's the fact that one of your people is still free and running around. Right now, I'm not particularly interested in tracking down Sloane. Are you, Agent McKenna?"

"No, not particularly."

"Right. However"—and now she did turn, and looked at Reagan with a terrifying coldness—"if you decide to let anyone in that building know who I am, I might be out of a job. That will give me all the time in the world to find Sloane and carve him into itty bitty pieces with my knives. My brother and I may not get along, but that doesn't mean I don't know as well as he does how long it takes a shade to die."

Reagan's jaw dropped. She looked at Alex. "Are you seriously going to let her say stuff like that?" she cried.

"Sure," he said easily, fighting down the lump of fear in his chest. "After all, we're just having a chat about hypotheticals. That's not a crime."

He climbed out of the SUV and went around to open the door nearest Reagan, putting his face dangerously close to her. "At the end of the day," he said softly, tilting his head toward Lindy. "I don't control her. I never did, and I never will. Might want to keep that in mind."

~

When he returned to the SUV, having passed a *very* quiet Reagan and Cooper over to the state police, Lindy was hunched in the passenger seat with her knees pulled to her chest. She didn't look at him as he climbed in and started the engine. He only broke the silence when he needed directions to drive her home.

Lindy had purchased a brownstone in Lincoln Park, just a couple of streets away from the Chicago History Museum. Alex hadn't actually been there before—he'd been traveling for the last few weeks, and she'd only just moved in—but he let out a low whistle when he saw the three-story brick building. He didn't even want to think about how much something like that would cost.

"You bought the whole thing?"

"It's best," she said, "for security purposes." She saw his obvious interest and smiled just a tiny bit. "Want to walk me in?"

The brownstone was just as beautiful on the inside as the outside, with wood floors and a brick fireplace that had to be original to the building. The upper stories were in the process of being renovated, Lindy explained—they had been cut up into separate apartments, and she was now trying to restore them to one residence—so she had to content herself with the single bedrooms and sunken living room on the ground floor.

"So you're like, stupid rich, huh?" Alex said, looking around. The only furniture in the living room was a red leather sofa, which looked the perfect amount of worn.

Lindy sat down at one end and curled her legs up beside her. "I guess so. It's not that hard, when you've been alive a few centuries." She shrugged. "And I've been alive a lot longer than that."

Still standing, Alex turned to look at her. It was just past midnight, still early for Lindy, but she looked haggard and anxious. Alex went and sat at the other end of the sofa. "Okay," he said, "what's bothering you *most*?"

She lifted her eyes to him. "Aren't you going to ask me if I'd really go after Sloane like that?"

"Nope."

"Why not?"

"Mostly it's an ego thing," he explained. "I'm way too full of myself to think that I could have misjudged you that badly."

A tiny smile appeared on her face. "What exactly are you trying to hide, when you do that 'swaggering Boy Scout' bit?"

"Naked fear that someone will realize I'm a fake," he said cheerfully. "Pretty much the same as everyone else." His face grew serious. "Look, Lindy, it was a good bluff, and I understood why you made it. If you're looking for judgment, I don't have any for you."

"What if it wasn't a bluff?" she challenged.

Alex sat down on the couch, studying her. "Sloane didn't lift a finger against you, even though it meant betraying his girlfriend. We both know you're not going to hurt him," he said matter-of-factly.

Her face softened, and Alex could practically see the weight lifting from her. "It's not just that, though," she said. "I've got this terrible feeling that everything we did today was exactly what Hector wanted us to do. Up to and including capturing Reagan."

"You think we played into his hand?"

"I think it's a good general rule to assume that at all times, yes."

Alex thought about that for a minute. "Maybe we did," he admitted. "You're on the good-guy team now, and we have to play by rules. Which means it's not that hard to predict what we're going to do."

"And he's still out there. Having a *great* time manipulating us."

Alex shrugged. "You told me today that Hector is a chess player. Now you're worried that he's five moves ahead of us, and we're basically screwed?"

She nodded, her hands clenched on her lap. Alex reached over and touched her arm, just for a second. Her fists began to uncurl. "Maybe you're looking at it wrong. Hector left you alone for *years*. He went after you to get your blood, and now he's got it—but he's still making the effort to mess with you. Do you know what that tells me?"

"What?"

"That he's scared," Alex stated. "You said yourself that he goes on about you not being a leader, not helping the shades. But you surprised him, truly surprised him, by signing on to work with us. I don't get the impression that Hector is a guy who's surprised all that often."

"No, he's not."

"You got to him, and he doesn't like that. If he went into hiding, even I have to admit we might never find him. But because you unnerved him, he's got to reach out and mess with you. And *that's* how we're going to get him." Ruefully, he added, "It's just probably not going to be tonight."

She smiled in an unguarded, genuine way that warmed every part of him. "Lindy . . . ," he began, but he had no idea how to finish it.

"I know," she said softly.

"You do?"

She nodded. "You want to kiss me, but you don't think it's a good idea. Because you're the boss, and I'm your underling, and because you're a human and I'm a shade...and because sometimes I scare you."

He felt it then, the weight of her loneliness, her distance. How many years had she kept herself in exile? He could see in that moment that she didn't have anyone at all in her life. And he couldn't stand it.

Alex reached out and wrapped his hands around her waist. She could have swatted him across the room, but instead she allowed herself to be pulled into his lap. "First," he said, "I would never use the word *underling*. It's so dated." She smiled, her hair forming a curtain around her face. "Second, I am not afraid of you."

"Maybe you should be," she whispered.

"That's my decision, and not yours."

Slowly, she brought her hands up to rest on either side of his face, and spoke into his mind. *Alex . . .*

His mouth surged up to meet hers.

Chapter 25

At eight a.m., someone banged hard on Lindy's front door.

Lindy had allowed herself to drift off to sleep. She could go without it, but she had felt warm and comfortable and at peace, for the first time in . . . well, a very long time. When the banging began, she sat bolt upright, instantly awake, though in her more weakened state. She hurried toward the front door, pulling on a robe as she walked.

The moment she opened the door, Chase Eddy burst through it. "I need to talk to Alex," he announced.

"Um, good morning, I guess. Why would you think—"

"I tracked his phone," Chase said shortly.

Alex came stumbling out of the bedroom still pulling his pants on over his boxer shorts, the long scar from his temple to his opposite shoulder looking angry against his

233

pale skin. "Hey, Chase. Uh . . ." He looked down at himself. "Well, this is exactly what it looks like."

"It doesn't matter. Why aren't you answering your phone?" He was pacing in short lines, anxious energy practically radiating off him. Lindy could smell his fear.

Alex looked surprised, although Lindy couldn't tell if it was because Chase didn't care about them sleeping together, or the question. He took the phone out of his pants pocket and looked at it, grimacing. "I didn't hear it. And I thought we had things under control for the night."

The energy seemed to leave Chase, and he sat down heavily on one end of the sofa. "Yeah. About that."

"What happened?" Lindy asked.

"I think . . . I think I fucked up really bad," he blurted.

"Isn't that kind of *my* job?" Alex said, offering a smile.

Chase didn't even respond. Alex sat down next to him. "What happened?"

"While you were still in the hospital, Lindy gave us this whole lecture on how to safeguard ourselves against shade attacks," Chase began, "and how to know if someone has taken our blood and erased our memory."

Lindy nodded, confirming it.

"Okay . . ."

"Last week, I realized that I was missing time. Only twenty minutes, here and there, but it was happening too often, nearly every day. I started to worry that I'd been compromised."

"Why didn't you say anything?"

"I . . . I don't know." The other agent looked anguished. "I somehow got this idea in my head that you and Lindy are bad for each other. You've always been like fuel, Alex," he said in a rush, before anyone could answer. "You make things happen. It's why you're a great agent, why I've always been happy to follow you. But Lindy . . ." He didn't look at her. She might as well have not even been in the room. "She's an explosive. Fuel and explosives, you see? I got this idea that by keeping my missing time a secret, I would help protect you from her."

Alex wasn't sure how to answer. Lindy said quietly, "The easiest way to mesmerize a human is to play on an emotion that's already there."

Alex nodded. "Protecting me is pretty much part of your genetic code at this point, dude."

Chase let out a broken laugh. "Except I didn't. Or I thought I was, but it was all fuzzy, and someone kept sort of erasing their tracks, and I couldn't keep anything in my *head* . . ."

"That sounds pretty sophisticated," Alex said in a neutral tone.

Lindy looked at him in horror. *Hector.*

For a moment, she could see all his moves laid out on

the board. Chase was second only to Alex in the Chicago BPI; he knew *everything*. Hector would love corrupting the SAC's best friend. Which would push Alex and Lindy closer together, distracting them both.

"Chase, what happened?" Alex asked, obviously trying to keep the panic out of his voice.

"Gil called me this morning," Chase whispered. "The van left at six a.m. Forty-five minutes ago, they were attacked. The shades are gone. Harvey Bartell is dead, and so is the kid that Gil sent with him."

"Oh, God." Lindy heard herself say. Bartell, who had been so kind to her. Hector had taken him. "Alex, you need to call—"

But his cell phone was already beginning to buzz in his hand. He looked at the screen and mumbled, "I've got to take this." He touched a button, and in a clearer voice, said, "Hello, Deputy Director. I just heard about the van."

Lindy was close enough to hear an exhalation, then the deputy director's voice said, "I'm sorry to say it, but we have bigger problems than that right now, Alex. Camp Vamp was just attacked. All the inmates have escaped."

ACKNOWLEDGMENTS

First and foremost: thank you so much to those of you who loved *Nightshades* and asked for more. My particular thanks to the Amazon reviewer who called it "*Criminal Minds* with vampires," because I haven't had to struggle to think up a logline since.

Thank you to Mr. Charles de Lint (does Canada have a knighthood program yet?) who read *Nightshades* and gave me a beautiful cover quote. Having a legend in urban fantasy on my cheering squad has humbled me more than I can say, and with every new book I write, my goal is to live up to what he thinks I can do.

I of course need to thank my husband, who accepts it when I say things like, "Dude, I gotta go do research in Chicago tomorrow. Watch the kids." Marriage is complicated and not always easy, but I am truly lucky to have a spouse who supports my career so thoroughly, whether it's watching the kids or helping me hash out Reagan's motivation while we walk on the track at the gym. His ideas are almost always terrible, God love him, but that often helps me see the right path by omission.

The village of Switch Creek is completely fictional, but

there are a few places mentioned in *Switchback* that are not. I have, as usual, taken liberties in terms of building layout, hours, security, etc., in the name of telling a better—and shorter—story. All inaccuracies are mine.

Finally, thank you to my editor at Tor.com, Lee Harris, who provides an excellent editorial eye along with his witty banter (or maybe vice versa?). Not everyone gets a boss who makes work fun, and to those people I say: suck it.

(Vampire humor.)

About the Author

Photograph by Elizabeth Craft

MELISSA F. OLSON is the author of the Scarlett Bernard series of urban fantasy novels, the Nightshades series, and the mystery *The Big Keep*.

She lives in Madison, Wisconsin, with her family and two comically oversized dogs.

TOR·COM

Science fiction. Fantasy. The universe.

And related subjects.

*

More than just a publisher's website, *Tor.com*
is a venue for **original fiction, comics,** and
discussion of the entire field of SF and fantasy,
in all media and from all sources. Visit our site
today—and join the conversation yourself.

CPSIA information can be obtained
at www.ICGtesting.com
Printed in the USA
LVHW04s1830280818
588393LV00004B/629/P